Spirit of the Northwest

Spirit of the Northwest

Charlotte Fox

Northwest Publishing, Inc.
Salt Lake City, Utah

Spirit of the Northwest

All rights reserved.
Copyright © 1995 Charlotte Fox

Reproduction in any manner, in whole or in part,
in English or in other languages, or otherwise
without written permission of the publisher is prohibited.

This is a work of fiction.
All characters and events portrayed in this book are fictional,
and any resemblance to real people or incidents is purely coincidental.

For information address: Northwest Publishing, Inc.
6906 South 300 West, Salt Lake City, Utah 84047
WC 8.29.95 /CA

PRINTING HISTORY
First Printing 1996

ISBN: 1-56901-477-9

NPI books are published by Northwest Publishing, Incorporated,
6906 South 300 West, Salt Lake City, Utah 84047.
The name "NPI" and the "NPI" logo are trademarks belonging to
Northwest Publishing, Incorporated.

PRINTED IN THE UNITED STATES OF AMERICA.
10 9 8 7 6 5 4 3 2 1

Special Acknowledgement

It is with the utmost love and gratitude that I recognize the love and support given me by my husband Doug and our daughter Amanda.

Charlie/Mom

Chapter One

Jeremy Bolt sat in his favorite chair on the front porch, coffee cup in hand, and surveyed the distant harbor city of Seattle. This had been his home for as long as he could remember. Now here it was, June 1889, and change had swept through the Washington territory like wildfire. Seattle, while not the capital, had probably progressed the most of all the other cities in the territory in the past twenty-odd years.

"You're up early," a young woman said softly. Jeremy's blue eyes smiled even before he did.

"Special day," he replied.

"I'm a little nervous," Kathryn Bolt stated, sitting beside her father.

"That's understandable." Jeremy blinked back his tears as he gazed in awe at his twenty-year-old daughter. Light blue eyes smiled back at him from a face framed by auburn locks. *Practically the spitting image of her mother*, Jeremy thought.

"What is it?"

"You remind me so much of your mother. You always have, but more so in the last year."

"I'm wearing Mother's wedding gown today."

"I know. I think she cried all night long!" They both laughed lightly at that. "I love you."

"I love you, too, Daddy." Kathryn leaned over and hugged her father, then stood. "Well, might as well get my bath before Jon gets in there with his menagerie! I swear he has more animals than Richard!"

"Well, he's at that age, I think. I seem to remember collecting lots of things when I was ten. At least…"

"What?"

"Nothing, j-just thinkin'."

"Childhood was hard for you, wasn't it?" Kathryn placed a gentle hand on her father's shoulder.

"At times," Jeremy confessed with a sigh. "Seems so long ago." He paused and chuckled. "A lot of years have passed!" He stood then and hugged his daughter once more. "No sad thoughts today. My little girl's gettin' married! Go on now before your brother beats you to the bathroom!"

"All right. You coming in?"

"In a little while. I think I'll let your mother sleep a little longer." Kathryn nodded and went back inside the house. Jeremy sighed again as his thoughts returned to his childhood. Stuttering had always put him at a disadvantage, even into adulthood. But Candy Pruitt, Mrs. Jeremy Bolt for more than twenty years now, had put an end to his self-pity. Jeremy smiled at that. His wife was a headstrong woman and probably always would be. He saw a lot of that in his daughter now, he realized. With a chuckle, he stepped off the porch and headed toward the coachhouse.

About an hour later, Jonathan practically burst into the building just as Jeremy put the finishing strokes on the brass trim. He turned around to face his son and grinned; Jonathan's face bore traces of syrup already.

"Breakfast is ready, I guess," Jeremy said.

"Yep! Good, too!"

"So I see." Jeremy tousled his son's dark hair and laughed. "Guess I better get cleaned up, huh?" Jonathan nodded and ran ahead of his father. Jeremy just shook his head. The screen door opened as they reached the house, and a beautiful, auburn-haired woman stepped out. Jeremy stopped and stared at this vision in front of him. *Is it possible that Candy hasn't aged in all these years?* he wondered. Her blue eyes were still just as bright and full of life as always. Her shining tresses bore only a wisp of gray.

"Breakfast," she called to him and smiled.

"Coming," Jeremy replied and quickly made up the distance to the house. Jonathan was already back inside. Jeremy embraced his wife, surprising her. Then his lips gently caressed hers as he stroked her soft hair. "I love you," he whispered.

"I love you, too." Candy's eyes glimmered with tears as she returned his kiss. "Feeling your oats today?" she asked with a devilish smile.

"Something...like that."

"Well, I better feed you, then!"

"Something smells good," Jeremy said, following Candy into the house. "I think I'd better hurry or our son will eat everything in sight!"

The scene was much the same at Joshua Bolt's home. His son, Richard, had quickly devoured his breakfast, which was nothing unusual. Blond like his father, Richard also had blue eyes that seemed to be a Bolt trait. But unlike his short cousin, Richard already stood over five feet, at ten years of age. But then, his father and Uncle Jason were both over six feet tall. His Uncle Jeremy, however, wasn't much taller than Richard.

"I'm goin' over to Jon's," Richard announced, but his father caught him at the door.

"Not today, boy," Joshua stated. He started to smile but a

warning glance from his wife stifled that. "Your cousin, Kathryn, is getting married this afternoon, so you have to stay clean."

"Ah, Dad," Richard whined.

"I'm sure Jonathan has to stay the same," Callie Bolt replied confidently.

"Probably more so," Joshua laughed, knowing his sister-in-law. "At least for today."

"All right," Richard said, dejected. Then a mischievous smile slowly curled his mouth upward. "Can I at least go outside?"

"All right, but remember what we said," his mother said. She looked at Joshua and, with a shake of her dark curls, smiled. Richard was the out the door before they knew it.

"He and Jon are sure alike," Joshua commented.

"Kind of like you and Jeremy?" his wife asked as she began cleaning up the breakfast dishes.

"Yeah, when *I* was the boys' age." A thoughtful look crossed Joshua's face and he sighed. "It wasn't but a year later that we lost Mom. After that, Jeremy didn't play too much...with me or any of his friends."

"That's when he began stuttering?"

"Yes. Well," he paused and grinned, "he met Candy just in time."

"I'm sure he's thankful that neither of their children have any problems."

"You can bet on that. Need any help?"

"Not yet. You can help your son dress later, all right?"

"All right," Joshua replied with a hearty laugh. "Think I'll go see Jason for a bit. I know I promised not to work today, but..."

"Oh, go on," Callie said, smiling. "You'd just be in my way here anyway." Joshua gave his wife a parting kiss, then left.

Joshua passed Jeremy's place on the way to their oldest brother's house. With a grin, he turned his horse around and decided that Jeremy might like to get away for a little bit. As he approached the two-story house, he knew he was right. Jeremy was out on the front stoop, polishing his boots.

"Hey there, Father of the Bride!" Joshua called as he dismounted.

"Josh!" Jeremy called out, smiling.

"Thought I'd come and rescue you." Both brothers laughed at that and nodded.

"I could use it. Women!"

"What about women?" Candy asked as she opened the screen door.

"Oh, nothing, uh, just, um," Jeremy stammered, flustered at getting caught.

"Oh, go on with Joshua," Candy stated impatiently. "I know you're just itching to get out of here for a while!"

"Well, I think I will," Jeremy replied, grinning. "I'll be back in plenty of time, don't worry."

"I won't, but Kathryn might."

"I won't be late, I promise. Not today. See you later." Jeremy mounted his already saddled horse...he'd planned to sneak away anyway.

"Say hello to Jason for me," Candy requested then went back inside the house.

"She knows you, Brother!" Joshua said with a laugh.

"Yeah, too well, sometimes," Jeremy muttered.

"Come on, Jason got those new railway plans drawn up."

Chapter Two

By early afternoon, despite the unusually hot temperature, most of Seattle seemed to be turning out for Kathryn Bolt's wedding. Kathryn had been born and raised in Seattle and knew most of the citizens. She'd only recently returned from being away at college for two years, where she had earned her teaching credentials. In the fall, she would take over the teaching post being vacated by a retiring schoolteacher, Essie Gustafson.

Steven Fairfield, a dark-haired and brown-eyed native of San Francisco, stood under the shade of big fir trees with his friends. The church, with its new coat of white, was only a few yards away and Steven nervously shifted from foot to foot.

"Uh-oh, here comes your father-in-law," Eugene Walker said in almost a whisper.

"I like Jeremy," Steven stated defensively.

"Yeah, well, you don't have to work for him," Walker replied.

"You never complained about him before. Why now?"

"Ah, he's just sore cause Mr. Bolt's been a little edgy," Buddy Ryan said.

"Well, Kathryn is his only daughter," Steven said with a smile. "I think I'd be a little edgy, too." The three friends laughed at that, and even Walker nodded.

"Afternoon, Mr. Bolt," Ryan said as Jeremy started past the younger men.

"Oh, hello," Jeremy replied and came over to the group.

"I'm a very lucky man," Steven said, still feeling a little awkward.

"Always remember that," Jeremy stated then chuckled. "Believe me, Kathryn won't ever let you forget it!"

"You don't seem quite so nervous today," Walker said quietly. Jeremy almost frowned then nodded.

"Sorry about the last couple of weeks, Gene, Buddy," he said. "It hasn't been just the wedding. My brothers and I are looking at plans to expand the operation. So, if I've been hard to get along with, I apologize."

"Understandable," Ryan replied, sticking out his hand to his boss. "Thanks for telling us, though." Jeremy shook his hand and looked at Walker expectantly.

"Yeah, thanks," the freckle-faced youth said but made no move to shake Jeremy's hand. Jeremy nodded then turned back to Steven.

"See you inside," he said and patted Steven's shoulder, then headed toward the church.

"Why didn't you shake his hand?" Steven asked Walker.

"Didn't want to," Walker answered with a shrug. "Think I'll go inside, too."

"I can see trouble brewing," Ryan said after Walker left. "Gene's never liked logging, but it's a job."

"Then he should find some other kind of work," Steven said.

"I think he wants to but his father's always worked for the Bolts, so Gene thinks he has to, too."

"Now that his father's dead…"

"I think that's the problem. Mr. Walker got killed on the job and Gene's still bitter."

"And afraid, maybe," Steven said thoughtfully. "I think I'll talk to him about coming to work for me. I probably won't be able to hire him until next year sometime, but maybe the prospect of a new kind of work will help."

"It sure couldn't hurt, I don't suppose. Well, you 'bout ready to go in and claim your bride?"

"Katy really is a terrific girl," Steven stated, grinning. "But she can be headstrong!"

"She gets that from her mother!" came the booming of Jason Bolt. The eldest of the Bolt brothers, Jason still struck a handsome profile with his dark, wavy hair, piercing blue eyes, and lean body that now towered over his new nephew.

"I'm glad that came from you and not me!" Steven said with a laugh.

"Seen your father-in-law yet?"

"Oh yes. He's already gone inside," Ryan said. "Think I'll head that way as well."

"Well, I think I'll accompany you, Steven," Jason said, putting an arm around Steven. "Make sure you don't make any wrong turns."

"Not me!" Steven said and both men laughed heartily.

Meanwhile, in the back room, inside the church, a jittery bride paced nervously as her mother calmly watched. Kathryn paused, looked at Candy and sighed. She knew she was ready for this marriage, and she did love Steven. But that didn't make her any less nervous.

"You're beautiful. Steven is getting a wonderful wife," Candy said softly, pressing her lips together to keep from crying.

"Oh, I don't know. I think he's gettin' a handful!" Jeremy chuckled as he came inside the room.

"Oh, Daddy!" Kathryn said with a laugh. Jeremy shook

his head as he surveyed the lovely vision in white.

"You *are* beautiful. Just as beautiful as your mother," he said, taking his daughter in his arms. "I...I can't believe you're grown up." Kathryn stepped back, smiling.

"Thank you." She started to say something else when the organ music began to play. Taking a deep breath, she finally spoke again. "Well, I guess this is it." She nervously fingered her hair as Candy pinned the veil in place.

"I'll see you in a little while," she whispered and both women exchanged brief hugs. "I love you," Candy said with a smile, then left.

"I'll j-just wait on you out here, all right?" Jeremy asked.

"All right. Thanks, Daddy."

Jeremy stood at the window, staring out at the sunny day outside. But his mind wasn't on the Seattle summer day. His daughter...his only daughter, was about to be married. *How could time have just flown by like this?* he wondered. It seemed like only yesterday she was climbing up into his lap and begging for a story.

"Where have the years gone?" he asked no one.

"Daddy?" Kathryn asked and Jeremy turned to face her, all smiles. "Oh, Daddy, don't be sad today."

"I'm not...I'm trying not to be," he replied. "I am happy for you." Kathryn blinked back her tears and smiled. The organ music changed suddenly and both father and daughter sighed. "This is it, honey," Jeremy said softly.

"I love you, Daddy."

"Well, shall we?" Kathryn put her hand on her father's arm and they went to their spot. As the bridal fanfare began, the bride and her father started the walk down the aisle. The wedding guests hushed as Jeremy finally put Kathryn's hand in Steven's.

"Who gives this woman?" the minister asked.

"I do," Jeremy replied then went to sit beside his wife. The minister began the ceremony, and Kathryn and Steven listened intently to every word. Although Reverend Jacobs wasn't a slow man by any means, his idea of marriage was to challenge not only the young couple before him, but those who were already married or contemplating being wed, which made for a lengthy speech. However, all things considered, he soon got to the heart of the ceremony.

"If there is anyone here who knows any reason why this man and this woman should not be joined in holy matrimony, let him speak now or forever hold his peace." The minister paused and a deadly silence filled the church. As the clergyman started to continue, a man in the back of the church stood up, causing heads to turn his way.

"I have a reason!" he bellowed. Jeremy immediately stood up, angered at the intrusion, but stayed put.

"And just the who the hell are you?" he asked loudly.

"Jeremy!" Candy exclaimed. Jeremy ignored his wife and went on.

"I asked you a question!"

The dark-haired, attractive man walked down the aisle, stopping in front of Jeremy before saying any more.

"I'm Jerome Douglas, Mr. Bolt. And I have several reasons concerning your daughter." Kathryn, in tears now, turned to her father.

"Daddy, I don't know what he's talking about!"

"Kat, how can you say that? After all the time you spent at my cabin," Douglas said, offended. Overcome by shock, Kathryn was momentarily speechless as Steven finally stepped forward.

"Mr. Douglas, can you support these accusations?" he asked.

"Steven!" Kathryn shouted, angry now. "How can you even ask that?"

"Katy, please, just let the man speak. Besides, I haven't known you all that long." Jeremy started forward but Candy pulled on his jacket. He turned her way, frowned, but remained quiet.

"You're right. You haven't. And now, Mr. Fairfield, you won't!" Kathryn yelled. She looked at her mother, tears rolling down her cheeks now, and rushed out of the sanctuary. Candy quickly went after her daughter. The minister turned to Jeremy and spoke softly.

"Mr. Bolt, may I suggest you men take this matter elsewhere?"

"Of course," Jeremy replied. "Gentlemen, shall we?"

"Certainly," Steven stated.

"I believe Kat should be involved in this as well," Douglas said, hesitating.

"Her name is Kathryn," Jeremy said heatedly. "And if *I* decide she should be, she will be. Let's go." Jeremy and Steven headed out the front door of the church, and Douglas followed, although a little more slowly. Jeremy pointed to a fairly isolated spot, just past where the horses and buggies were tethered. As Douglas passed several of the horses, he suddenly leaped on one, apparently his own horse, making good his escape before either Jeremy or Steven had time to react. As they watched Douglas disappear, Jeremy turned to Steven.

"Now what do you believe? Or who?" he asked, still angry.

"Jeremy, I'm...confused," Steven replied, bewildered. "Please try to see it from my side. I have no idea what Kathryn was like before I met her." He held up a hand when Jeremy made a move to interrupt. "Please, hear me out. I think she and I both need time to really think about our relationship now."

"Yes, I think you do," Jeremy sighed. "I will tell you this much: my daughter has been brought up with proper values. And I know her well!"

"But you weren't with her those two years she was away at school."

"Maybe not, but...never mind. I think it best if you don't come around my family for a while."

Steven nodded then headed for his own horse. Jeremy shook his head. He had come to like Steven, and deep down inside, Jeremy understood the young man's confusion. Sighing again, he started back toward the church. A hurt and angry young woman needed him now.

Jeremy quietly walked inside the church and paused just outside the little room where, just a short time ago, there had been laughter and tears of happiness. Now, all he could hear were muffled sobs. As soon as Kathryn saw her father, she rushed to his arms.

"Oh, Daddy!" she sobbed.

"It'll be all right. Hush now. Don't you worry," he said quietly.

"I can't believe this is happening!"

"Yeah, I know. Neither can I." He put her at arm's length, then said, "Come on and sit with me. I know this is gonna be hard to talk about, but we need to." Kathryn nodded and sat beside her father. Candy sat down as well, remaining quiet for the moment. Jeremy took a deep breath and blew it out. "Now," he continued, "talk to me about Jerome Douglas."

"Well, there's not really a whole lot to tell," Kathryn began, sniffling. "He was a guest lecturer at school for a while. The dean had invited him because of his background in criminal law. I think he used to work with federal marshals.

"Anyway, I found him interesting…his talks, I mean. He took a liking to me and I did have a few talks with him. But never alone!"

"Why would he come all this way just to ruin your wedding? How would he have even known you were getting married?" Jeremy asked, surprising even himself with his calmness.

"I…I wrote to him a couple of times after I came home. I never received any replies and I forgot all about him."

"All right," Jeremy sighed, "he knew where you lived. But that still doesn't explain why he would come all this way just to upset the wedding. Is there something you're not telling me?"

"Yes." Kathryn paused, tearful again. "He used to send me flowers a lot and other gifts. It was all very proper, though. He was always a gentleman. I returned all the gifts and he finally quit sending them. And he remained friendly but not overly so."

"Kathryn, why didn't you tell us about him?" Candy finally asked. Kathryn looked directly at her father before answering.

"I knew Daddy would do something...fatherly!" Jeremy's mouth dropped open. "Oh, don't look so shocked!" Kathryn stated. "You would have made a special trip to get me. And I didn't want to come home. Besides, I never felt threatened in any way. I guess I didn't think I was in any kind of danger."

"Well, you're right about one thing," Candy said, "your father would have come after you!"

"Hey, I'm not the bad guy here!" Jeremy defended himself. "Look, what's done is done. We'll find Douglas and get him to tell Steven the truth...that nothing improper ever happened. Douglas is obviously jealous." He paused and shook his head, grinning. "I never thought I'd hear myself say that about my daughter." They all laughed at that. Jeremy sighed and patted Kathryn's hands and smiled. "Don't worry, everything will work out. You stay here with your mother for a while, all right? I'll go get rid of the guests. I love you, honey."

"Thank you, Daddy. I love you, too. Thanks for believing in me."

"There was never any doubt." Jeremy started out when Kathryn suddenly remembered something.

"Wait, Dad! I don't know a lot about Douglas' background but I heard things about him. He's dangerous."

"What kind of things?" Candy asked.

"He's real good with guns."

"All right. I stand warned. It'll be all right," Jeremy replied. Kathryn nodded and even managed a smile for her father. He nodded in return, then left.

Jeremy quietly asked the wedding guests to leave. He announced that there would be no wedding that day. There were some things that the family had to take care of, he explained. And he apologized for the unexpected outburst. Friends and family alike streamed out of the church, respectful of the father's request. Jeremy sat down then, and his brothers joined him.

"Jeremy, does Kathryn know Douglas?" Jason asked, patting Jeremy's shoulder.

"Says she does…met him at school. But he took off before I could ask him anything else, which only confused Steven more. I gotta admit, I'm confused, too."

"Jeremy, you know Kathryn hasn't done anything wrong…well, not really wrong, but…" Joshua faltered.

"Josh, I know what you mean. And I intend to find Douglas and see just what he means."

"Well, you know we'll do all we can to help," Jason offered.

"I know, Jason, thanks. Poor Kathryn, she—"

The sudden flinging of the church doors interrupted Jeremy. A man, covered with soot, rushed down the aisle toward the Bolt brothers. Jason grabbed him and tried to get him to sit down, but the man, practically breathless, refused.

"Seattle's on fire!" he shouted. "We need everyone! Hurry!" He then ran back out of the church. Too stunned to say anything, all three brothers rushed out as well.

Chapter Three

By the time the Bolt brothers reached the outskirts of the city, Seattle's waterfront had practically disappeared from sight. Dark, billowing smoke made it hard to see what was ablaze and what wasn't. Other citizens arrived about the same time as Jason, Joshua, and Jeremy. The shock on their faces gave way to determination...they would fight very hard to save their city.

As people hurriedly joined the firefighting efforts already underway, the scene quickly became a sort of organized chaos. Firefighters rushed around with waterhoses, spraying everywhere they could see flames. The continued onrush of smoke, however, made it hard to tell where to aim the precious water.

Men's jackets and ties were tossed aside as they

courageously battled the fire. It seemed almost hopeless, for as soon as one fire was put out, another sprang up nearby. The townspeople fought on, undaunted. The unusually dry, hot weather further hampered efforts.

By early evening, tents had been erected on hilltops which were some distance from the fire. Since there was always a danger of the flames spreading out that far, being that fire would spread much quicker going uphill, mobility was the key. And everyone involved was prepared to move at a moment's notice.

There were now facilities for medical treatment, food, and rest. Women had been hauling in supplies and food all afternoon and even children had pitched in to help where they could. Candy and Kathryn helped set up one of the food tents and quickly went about the task of seeing that those fighting the overwhelming blaze were taken care of. Candy practically preached to them that they had to take breaks. The doctors and nurses had wholeheartedly agreed with her and others who had been trying to get the firefighters to work in shifts.

When Jeremy walked inside the food tent, he had to smile. His wife and daughter were busily serving up food and drink as the workers finally began filing in. Candy looked his way and managed a smile in spite of everything. Her hair, though mostly still arranged on top of her head, was practically plastered to her face and neck, but Jeremy thought his wife was more beautiful than ever. He even grinned as he quickly made his way to her.

"It's pretty bad, isn't it?" she asked as she wiped some of the soot off Jeremy's face.

"Yeah. It's going to take every man in Seattle to put this one out, I think. Whoever set it—"

"You think Jerome Douglas did it, don't you?" Kathryn asked, interrupting.

"Maybe," Jeremy sighed. "I just don't know. He certainly makes a good suspect. Jason, Josh, and I are going to look for him as soon as we can. But with this fire—"

"How about some water?" Candy asked, interrupting. "You look like you could use some."

"Thanks." Jeremy took the cup Candy offered and drained it. "Got any more?" Candy filled the cup and Jeremy took a couple of drinks, then handed the cup back to Candy. "Well, guess I better get back. It's going to be a long day." He started to leave but turned back to his wife. "Don't worry," he added and gave her a quick kiss.

"Please be careful," she said. "I know you will, but I just had to say it."

"And not just around the fire," Kathryn put in. "Douglas—"

"I'll be careful," Jeremy promised, grinning. "See you later." Mother and daughter exchanged doubtful looks as they watched Jeremy leave. He was right, though; it would be a long day.

Jeremy passed Steven on his way back down the hill. The two men looked at one another for only a moment, then went on. Jeremy got about a foot, sighed, and turned back around. The two almost collided as Steven, it seemed, had the same thought. Jeremy grinned in spite of everything that had happened.

"We could use you," he said.

"Thanks." No more was said as they hurried toward the heart of the firefighting efforts. Jeremy joined his brothers while Steven went with another group of men. The plan, the fire chief explained, was to start trying to divert the fire away from the areas not yet affected. Shovels were soon scraping away debris, or tilling the dry earth as it were. If the fire had no fuel, it would be easier to control, or would burn itself out if the firebreak was successful. The problem was that the heat was extremely intense, and smaller fires continued to spark. Several businesses had already been destroyed as the flames threatened to engulf the entire waterfront district.

Sawmill owner Aaron Stempel, his normally well-groomed appearance now wet and grimy like everyone else's, came rushing up to Jason. The roar of the flames made it hard to hear and Stempel had to stand close to be heard.

"I need your help, Bolt! My house…," he shouted. Jason nodded.

"Let's go!" he yelled then ran to where Joshua and Jeremy were clearing the charred remains of a building. "Josh! Jeremy!" he shouted. "Stempel's house is in the path of the fire! I'm goin' to help him!"

"We'll be fine here! Go on!" Joshua replied loudly, wiping his forearm across his sweat- and dirt-streaked face. Jason and Stempel hurried on toward the north end of the city. Joshua turned back to his work when he saw a man near the courthouse, with what looked like a torch in his hand. Joshua squinted to get a better look at the man, then grabbed Jeremy's shoulder, startling him.

"Jeremy! There's someone over there!" Josh yelled, pointing toward the courthouse. "He had a torch!" Jeremy's eyes scoured the area by the building but he saw no one.

"Do you see him now?" he asked loudly.

"No! But I know I did!"

"You wanna check it out?"

"Let's go!" Jeremy dropped his shovel and ran behind his brother, carefully skirting the spreading flames. The courthouse seemed intact when they reached it. Just then, Joshua thought he heard something. Jeremy nodded as he heard it, too. As they started around behind the building, glass shattered just above them as flames suddenly billowed out a window. Both men crouched quickly, covering their heads with their arms as the glass fell all around them.

"You all right?" Joshua asked as he cautiously stood up. He carefully shook bits of glass off his shirt.

"Yeah. Looks like you were right," Jeremy stated. As he gently tugged at his shirt to remove any glass, he noticed something on the ground. He knelt down and picked up the object. "Someone *was* here!" he shouted and showed the burnt-out torch to his brother. "C'mon! He can't be far!"

"Wait!" Joshua yelled. "Let me go back and get a couple of guns. This guy might be armed."

"All right. I'll move up a little...get away from the fire."
"Be right back!"
As Joshua rushed off, Jeremy slowly went up the road, still staying behind the buildings there. Finding what looked to be like a safe spot to wait for Joshua, Jeremy continued to watch for anything unusual.

Suddenly, a man stepped out from behind one of the buildings just a few yards away. He was visible only for a moment, but Jeremy saw him well enough to identify Jerome Douglas. Jeremy didn't stop to think about being careful, but ran after Douglas. The taller man quickly outdistanced him and had soon vanished again. A thin layer of smoke hung over the area and made it hard to breathe, let alone run very far. Jeremy knew the chase would have to be put off for now.

"Damn it!" he swore and kicked at the street. Another explosion caught his attention and he quickly went to a safer spot, deciding to wait for Joshua before going any farther.

"Jeremy!" Joshua yelled and sighed with relief when he finally spotted his brother. "What's wrong?" he asked as he handed Jeremy a pistol.

"I saw Douglas. I tried to chase him, but he got away," Jeremy replied, agitated.

"Well, we're gonna have to look for him later. The south firebreak isn't holding. We need to get back there and help." He placed a comforting hand on his brother's shoulder. "We'll find Douglas, Jeremy. Sooner or later!"

"All right. You're right," Jeremy conceded, nodding.

"Right! C'mon!" They quickly backtracked to where the firefighters were combating the spreading blaze.

Meanwhile, Jason had been helping Stempel with his house. Along with others, they were putting wet blankets on the outside of the house.

"Well, what do you think, Bolt?" Stempel asked as he stepped back to rest for a moment.

"Brilliant strategy!" Jason exclaimed and patted Stempel's shoulder. "It's gonna take a lot more blankets than this, though."

"I know. Thanks for helping."

"You'd have done the same for me." Jason turned and looked back toward the heart of the city.

"I know, Jason," Stempel said quietly. He and Jason exchanged grim glances. They had been an instrumental part of Seattle's history and its growth. They knew that their memories might be all that would be left of Seattle now.

"Let's hope the water holds out," Jason stated.

"No reason why it shouldn't. Guess the new water line got finished just in time, huh?" Stempel paused as other people began showing up with more blankets. Even some of the local Indians offered their own to help.

"Back to work!" Jason said and did just that. As they worked, it was easy to recall some of Seattle's beginnings.

Chapter Four

A group of rugged-looking men hurried through the mud that doubled as the main street on their way out of town. Trouble had been brewing and now it had come to a head. One of the loggers had gotten himself into a sticky mess and was about to be jailed by Aaron Stempel, sawmill owner and self-appointed lawkeeper.

Jason Bolt busily sawed at the mighty fir then noticed men below him yelling and waving their arms to get his attention. Having just topped the tree, Jason shimmied to the ground in record time. The men—his men—were talking at once and Jason had to yell.

"All right! All right! What's this all about?" he asked. "We're behind schedule as it is!"

"It's your brothers," Corky Masters stated. "There's talk

in town about stringin' somebody up." Jason did not wait for the short, stocky logger to say more. His long stride soon gave way to a full run, leaving the others far behind. They soon rallied, however, and followed down the side of Bridal Veil Mountain, site of the Bolt Brothers logging operation.

By the time Jason's moccasin-style boots hit Seattle's familiar muddy streets, he began yelling his brothers' names at the top of his lungs. As he looked around on his way in, he saw no one and heard nothing for several minutes.

"Joshua! Jeremy!" he called again, a worried look creasing his handsome brow. Worry gave way to relief as his younger brothers finally came into view, running toward the eldest of the family. Jason immediately put his arms around both men, a smile on his face. "Corky said you were in trouble."

"No, it's not us. It's one of the men," Joshua replied.

"It's Big Sw-Swe—" Jeremy began but Joshua finished. "Big Swede. They're gonna put him in the poky."

"What for?" Jason asked.

"We don't know," Joshua stated with a shrug. He turned around just to in time to see the other loggers running to catch up. Needless to say, everyone was glad to see that both younger Bolt brothers were alive and well. A look of anger and determination crossed Jason's face as he started toward the jail, his brothers and men in tow. On their way, they passed the totem pole in the town square from which hung a sign that read:

SEATTLE

POPULATION 152

Aaron Stempel, aristocratic as ever, was just about to toss Olaf "Big Swede" Gustafson into the town jail. Jason and his group arrived on the spot before that could be done, though.

"Stempel!" Jason shouted. "I told you—keep your hands off my men!"

"And I told you, sooner or later, one of your men is gonna wind up in there," Stempel stated, nodding toward the jail.

"For what?"

"A criminal attack on one of our women."

"Attack?" Jason asked, puzzled. "Big Swede, why he's too dumb to hurt a fly. Who'd he attack?"

"Me," said a soft voice. Jason's puzzlement gave way to disbelief.

"Miss Essie?" he asked. He looked at tall, burly, blue-eyed Big Swede who smiled in the schoolteacher's direction. "Her? Why, ya big dumb cheesebrain!"

"I was drunk, Jason," Swede admitted.

"Oh then, he was drunk," Jason stated nonchalantly.

"Does that excuse him?" Stempel asked and nodded to the jailer who put Swede behind bars. Jason grinned then and turned back to Essie.

"Miss Essie, I want you to tell us, right out, just tell us, what happened," he said.

"Well, I...I wasn't expecting anyone to come calling. I was just sitting there, grading the children's papers. And if I were expecting a gentleman—"

"You wouldn't have minded a bit," Jason interrupted.

"Let her talk for herself," Stempel said.

"Would you, Miss Essie?" Jason asked, smiling.

"No, but...he was so unmannerly; he just came to my back door and yanked my little bell!"

"Yanked your little bell, did he?" Jason asked, trying not to laugh.

"And...and when I saw him standing there, I pulled my camisole together like this," Essie went on, pulling her shawl closer together, "and he reached out and grabbed my hand."

"Now, how did that big monster grab your little hand, Miss Essie?" Jason asked, gently taking her hand in his. His over-six-foot frame literally towered over the shy woman, who was smiling now. "Like this?"

"Rougher than that." Jason pulled Essie close to him.

"Like this, huh? And what did that big monster do next?

Try to put his arm around you...like this?" Jason slid his arm around the beaming schoolteacher.

"Something like that," she replied with a light laugh.

"And what did that...man do next? Try to kiss you?" Jason's voice changed to a whisper with his next words. "Like this?" he asked as he lightly touched his lips to Essie's forehead. She was so overcome, she practically fainted in Jason's arms. "Easy, Miss Essie, easy," Jason said quietly, holding onto her. "That wasn't so terrible, was it?"

"Well, no, I don't...I don't know why I screamed. I just screamed and everybody started running, making a fuss." Jason stayed close to Essie as if his next words were meant only for her, not the crowd gathered all around them.

"The Big Swede's bashful, Miss Essie. As bashful as you are."

"Well, he was drunk," she stated.

"Maybe he had to get drunk to get up his courage to come callin'." Jason smiled at her as a look of enlightenment crossed her face, and she nodded.

"Let him out, Aaron," she said. Stempel stared blankly at her, unmoving.

"Let him out, Aaron," Jason repeated, a smug look on his face.

"Let him out," Stempel said finally, disgusted. The men started cheering as Swede stepped out of the jail.

"All right, all right, all right!" Jason shouted. "Up the mountain. Gettin' to be sundown, and we're fifty trees behind time." Then he turned to the Swedish lumberman. "And you, ya big lunkhead, next time you pull a fool trick like that—"

"Ain't gonna be no next time," Swede interrupted.

"That's right, there ain't," Jason agreed as he started to walk away with Joshua and Jeremy right beside him.

"'Cause I'm quittin'." Swede's words stopped the Bolts dead in their tracks and all three turned back around. "I can't stand it here anymore," Swede explained, his accent fitting his nickname. "All men, no women. I gotta go someplace where there's women, Jason."

"Where's that, Big Swede?" Jason asked calmly. Several loggers, including Swede, began suggesting different places, but mainly San Francisco.

"Hey now, hold on," Joshua said loudly, anger showing in his clear blue eyes. "Corky, Sam, McGee...don't we treat you right?"

"Oh sure ya do, Josh," Sam stated. "But when a guy starts gettin' all head up just lookin' at an old maid schoolteacher, he's crackin' up!"

"And it's time to quit," McGee added. The others began talking at once again, uttering phrases like, "C'mon, let's get outta here," and, "San Francisco, here we come!" But Jason stopped them cold.

"Now wait!" he shouted. "Wait a minute! If it's women ya want..."

"Yeah!"

"If it's women you want, I'll get 'em for ya!" Jason stated.

Jason, Joshua, Jeremy, and several other loggers stormed into Lottie's Saloon. Lottie Hatfield, the blond-haired, blue-eyed owner of the establishment turned their way and smiled. It was a little early in the day, but with the Bolt's men, nothing was very surprising.

"Lottie, I think you're gonna take this sitting down!" Jason stated, pulling up a chair for her. Lottie smiled and sat down, her fancy dress rustling as she did so. "Lottie, you're gonna be the richest woman in the Northwest."

"I am?"

"Yes! You and me, we're goin' into business."

"We are?"

"We are! I'm goin' down to San Francisco and I'm bringing me back a passel of girls." The other men cheered.

"What're you gonna do with them?" Lottie asked, which brought laughter from the men.

"Well, the first thing I'm gonna do, I'm gonna let you hire them."

"Oh, I see. You think I'd like to hire a bunch of fancy

ladies, do you?"

"You wouldn't?" Jason asked, bewildered.

"Nope! Somebody else tried it and they were run out of town by Aaron Stempel. So long, boys," Lottie replied. She got up and headed for the staircase. Jason followed her as the other men began talking at once.

"Oh, Lottie, Lottie, you gotta take a chance. Lottie, you gotta take a chance!" Jason shouted. "Why, I'll be right at your side every minute. You just think of it, Lottie. This place…Lovely Lottie's Garden of Eden of girls, Lottie, girls! Every place you throw your shoe!" Jason's blue eyes danced with excitement as his scheme came together in his head. Lottie just shook her head at his boyish enthusiasm. Jason Bolt was usually the mature type; after all, he was in his thirties. But he wasn't so mature now.

"They'll be swinging their fancy legs from the top of the grand piano," Jason went on, undaunted. "They'll be swinging like crystals from the chandelier, like ripe fruit from the summer trees. Shake 'em down, boys, shake 'em down! Grab yourself a peach, a pear, a wild plum. Squeeze 'em, bite 'em, fruit for every guy in town…no guy ever has to go hungry again!" He went back to stand in front of Lottie. "And you, Lottie, you'll be coming down that staircase, a little crown on your head. Lovely Lottie, Queen of the Fancy Ladies!" The men cheered again, excited. "How about it, Lottie?"

"You're acting like a fool," she replied.

"Why now, Lottie, you listen while the fool speaks. It's women we want and it's women we're goin' to get, right, men? And we know the kind of women we want, right, men?" But no one answered as Big Swede and others looked toward the front as Miss Essie Gillis entered. She shyly came forward and stopped in front of Swede.

"Mr. Bolt said you were bashful and I do think you are, so *I* came to talk to *you*. I'm sorry if I caused you any trouble. I'd like to beg your pardon. And I thought, Jason's right, it *is* spring. Till you came callin', I hadn't noticed. And I thought, if you'd like to take a walk, the sun's goin' down. It'll be a lovely evening." Her invitation given, Essie stood back.

"I'd...I would like that, Miss Essie," Swede replied, almost as shyly as Essie talked. He offered her his arm and she smiled as she placed her small hand there. They started to leave but Swede turned back around. "And I ain't drunk, either." No one uttered a word as they left. Lottie nodded her head knowingly.

"You understand now, Jason?" she asked. "Real men want real women, not floozies." The men started talking at once again, but Jason quieted them.

"Let her talk!" he yelled, then turned back to Lottie. "Go on, Lottie."

"Thank you, Jason. Now I'll tell you what you do. You get yourselves some respectable women. Women who want to get married. Those are the kind you need." Before she could go on, the men started their uproar again. Lottie raised her voice in order to be heard. "And you're not goin' to find 'em in San Francisco, but I'll tell you where you will find them."

"Where?" one man asked.

"New England," she replied, looking at Jason. "There's been a war, Jason. And lots of women have been left without men. Not the fancy ones, but the plain ones...the marrying kind." Jason thought for a moment and nodded. A terrible civil war had just ended and thousands of men from both the North and South had been killed.

"Gentlemen, she's right," Jason stated.

A short time later, the word had been spread all over Seattle that Jason Bolt had an expedition planned, and that its purpose was to bring back women from New England. Most of the townsfolk agreed that the town needed more people— women—to help the town grow. And most of them were willing to put in their own money, some of it being everything they had.

"I'd give my savings to bring some women here," one woman stated as a crowd stood outside Lottie's Saloon. The Bolt brothers listened quietly while the townspeople talked amongst themselves. Aaron Stempel, having been notified about what was going on in town, came busting in the midst of the throng, a wary eye on Jason Bolt.

"Hold it, now, hold it! Quiet down!" he shouted and everyone did so. "Have you all gone crazy? Throwing your money away on a man who's given this town nothing but trouble?"

"Women'll make the town grow," argued one woman. Other voices piped up in agreement.

"All right, all right," Stempel said, thoughtful. "Well, maybe you're right. What this town needs is women...help the town grow...be good for business...and more money for my sawmill." He paused and turned to Jason. "All right, Bolt. But a trip like this is gonna take a lot of money. Add up everything they've offered you. It won't be nearly enough. I'll tell you what I'll do. I'll make up the difference if you'll sign a contract."

"What contract, Stempel?" Jason asked as he crossed his arms.

"Well, how many bachelors you figure we got here?"

"Oh, maybe ninety, ninety-five."

"All right, let's make it a round number. You bring back one hundred girls, no less. Agreed?"

"Agreed."

"And no tramps, no tramps. We'll hold you to that. These girls have gotta be—well...clean, upright, respectable—"

"Marriageable," a woman stated.

"Right," Stempel said, smiling. "Marriageable. Agreed?"

"I agree to that," Jason replied. The men behind him murmured excitedly.

"And that's not all," Stempel went on. "Now, we don't want 'em running off the minute they see the place. So you gotta agree to keep 'em here for one whole year."

"I agree to that."

"Now, what if you fail?"

"I won't fail." Jason's face and voice were filled with confidence, but he realized what Stempel was really leading up to.

"What if you do? What have you lost? Nothing. Look at these people...risking every dollar of their savings. What are you risking?"

"What do you want me to risk, Stempel? Bridal Veil Mountain?"

"What else have you got?"

"Nothing," Jason admitted.

"Well?"

"Well, I don't own it all by myself. My brothers, Joshua and Jeremy, they own part of it, too."

"Well, ask 'em." Jason sighed and turned around.

"Joshua, Jeremy," he called as he quickly walked away from the crowd. His brothers followed him to almost the edge of the water. Jason gazed wistfully at the landscape in the distance.

"The mountain," he said. Joshua and Jeremy looked toward the snow-capped peak. "It's ours. It's all we got."

"The folks g-g-gave up everything for it, Jason," Jeremy said. The three brothers were all that remained of the Bolt family in the Northwest. And Bridal Veil Mountain and the logging operation there had been their parents' dream...theirs, too.

"It's our home, Jason," Joshua said.

"I know," Jason replied with a sigh. "So, what do you say? Do we take on Stempel or not?"

"I say yes, take him on," Joshua stated with a determined grin.

"Jeremy, how do you vote?" Jason asked. Jeremy seemed uncertain at first, then looked at Joshua, who nodded.

"I v-v-v, I vo-vo—" he began.

"Take it easy," Jason said softly, a hand on his youngest brother's shoulder. Jeremy had stuttered ever since their mother's death when Jeremy was just a child. And now, at almost twenty, it was hard for Jason and Joshua, who was twenty-five, to not try to shelter Jeremy. Despite his speech problem, however, Jeremy was just as stubborn as his brothers, with a temper to match.

"Yes!" he answered, excited.

"I vote yes, too," Jason said, smiling. They turned around and went back to Stempel and the others. "Stempel! You've got yourself a contract."

Stempel could hardly believe what he was hearing…the Bolts risking their very livelihood for what Stempel considered a pipe dream. Jason turned to his men then.

"Men, as of today, you're all engaged to be married!"

The men all cheered and people began talking at once, as Stempel slowly walked toward the water's edge. It was his turn to gaze out at Bridal Veil Mountain, but not wistfully; he was certain that he would soon be the new owner.

Chapter Five

After several weeks of traveling across country by stage and train, the three Bolt brothers definitely preferred the train. They didn't have ample time to take in many sights; they were in a hurry to reach New England. Lottie had given them names of several small towns, and they'd tried to find out as much as they could about them as well as others.

By the time they arrived on the eastern seaboard, Jason had decided on a small city in Massachusetts—New Bedford. It was a small but well-established town with a real government, run mostly by women. The real draw to this town over some of the others was that its female population outranked the male almost twenty to one—just the numbers the Bolts were hoping for. And hopefully, they'd be able to talk at least one hundred unattached young ladies to make new homes in Seattle.

"Well, I spoke with the skipper. He said we should arrive sometime tomorrow morning," Jason said. They'd managed to book passage from Washington City to New Bedford. "I think we selected the right city, boys. New Bedford is what I see Seattle being in a few years." Joshua sat up too fast in his bunk and smacked his head on the overhead.

"I'll never get used to traveling on a ship," he said with a laugh.

"Glad I d-don't have that pr-problem," Jeremy joked.

"Being the shortest has some advantages, huh?" Jason laughed and Jeremy nodded, lying back. He sighed heavily as Jason got ready for bed. "How's the stomach?" he asked Jeremy.

"F-Fine...now. As long as I don't h-have to look at the w-water."

"How're you gonna make the trip back by boat?" Joshua said, smiling. "It's a good six-month voyage."

"J-Jason, why-why do we, uh, have to g-g-go back to Seattle by sh-sh-boat?"

"Well, Jeremy, how would you propose we take one hundred women home?" Jason asked, sitting down.

"Well, I'm not-I'm not sure. S-Same way we came?"

"Oh, come on," Joshua began.

"Wait a minute, Josh," Jason interrupted. "All right, Jeremy, let's say we do. You think about exactly how we've been traveling." Jeremy frowned and nodded.

"Pr-Pretty rough."

"Right. These females are probably used to more comfortable accommodations."

"Right," Jeremy murmured. Jason slapped his youngest brother's leg and laughed.

"You're always thinkin'! That's good." Jeremy grinned at that.

"Think we'll have trouble, Jason?" Joshua asked.

"It's hard to say. I'd say if these women want to ever marry, we've got just as much to offer them as anyone else. I'd say it looks promising. We've heard so much about the large numbers of single females going west as mail-order brides.

"Our biggest problem is gonna be gettin' a ship. I know we've got a writ from President Johnson to secure one, but since the war, ships have been scarce."

"What about this one?" Joshua asked.

"No good. Hunter's got more work than he can handle now. I offered him the full twenty thousand dollars. No, boys, we've just got to hope for the best. First things first...get the women!"

By late morning, the Bolts were ready to descend on New Bedford's citizenry. They needn't have worried about what kind of reception they would receive. The three brothers, clad in their Sunday finest and each very attractive in his own right, turned heads as they walked into the very heart of the bustling seaport. Jason couldn't help but envy those who had founded such a wonderful city. He imagined what was in store for Seattle.

"Men!" several young ladies screamed as Jason, Joshua and Jeremy strolled around. Within minutes, they were besieged by women, young and old. Jason could hardly speak and finally opted not to. The three men distributed handbills they'd had printed up in Washington City.

They'd spent part of the night before writing in the day and time of the meeting they were going to hold. Jeremy had asked where they would be able to hold it; Jason answered, "Every well-run city has a town hall, right?" New Bedford definitely had one.

Passing out handbills as they went along, the men wondered if they'd have enough to give everyone. It was obvious that there would be quite a gathering at the meeting. Jason noticed a prominent building close to the waterfront and headed toward it. It read: "New Bedford Fire Department."

As they entered, someone was practically immersed, head first, in the smokestack of the fire engine. Another person, clad in men's trousers, shirt, and knit cap was bent over the brass runners, cleaning.

"Excuse me, boy. Mind if we hang this on your engine?" Joshua asked, handbill at the ready.

"I'm not a boy," the woman stated as she stood and faced the men.

"And you can't hang that thing on her engine," Jason remarked, a sly grin on his face.

"Gee, miss, you sure got a nice engine," Joshua murmured. The woman took the handbill from Joshua, dipped it into a barrel of water, then placed it back into Joshua's hand. "What's the matter, miss?" he asked. "Don't you want to get married?"

"I *am* married and I hate men," she retorted, then stalked out of the engine house. The person cleaning the smokestack popped up, excited. She removed her cap and shook out her long, auburn tresses, her blue eyes twinkling.

"I don't hate men. I love 'em! And I'm gonna snag one with my bare hands. What time's the meeting?"

"Seven o'clock sharp," Joshua said and gave her a handbill. As she read over the paper, three other women came in through the front door of the firehouse. They seemed to be upset about something, then one pointed to the Bolts.

"There they are—the ones we should talk to about this. They're the ones, right there," she said.

"Go on, ask 'em," one of the others whispered. The men went over to find out what was wrong. Biddie Cloom, the woman who seemed a little more vocal than the others, spoke again.

"Is this true? What this says?" she asked, holding up the handbill. "Is it all true? We don't understand the little print."

"Little print?" Jason asked, putting an arm around Biddie. "Miss, you don't have to read the little print. You can read our faces. Haven't we got honest faces?"

"Don't we look like the kind *you* can trust?" Joshua added.

"Haven't we got the bluest eyes you ever saw?" Jason asked, looking deeply into Biddie's wide eyes. Jeremy shook his head. His brothers would win these women over, he thought.

"And we trust you?" Joshua asked.

"And we like you?" Jason went on.

"And we do like you," Joshua affirmed.

"Then why don't you like us?" Jason asked, feigning hurt. Biddie's eyes widened even further.

"Oh, I do, I do!" she exclaimed, smiling.

"See you at the meetin'...seven o'clock!" Jason stated, walking away.

"I'll be there at a quarter of five!" Biddie shouted, excited all over again. She and her companions giggled as they left the building. The woman on the smokestack, who'd been quietly listening to the conversation, threw her handbill at Jason as she jumped off the fire engine.

"What did you do that for?" Jason asked, puzzled.

"Well, you sure had me fooled," she said. "I thought you meant it. Every word on that handbill. But that line of fast talk you gave those girls...you're nothin' but razzle dazzlers. And when I go to that meetin' tonight, you'd better be prepared to answer a whole lot of questions." She strutted off and left Jason and Joshua stunned.

"That girl's gonna stay a fireman for the rest of her life," Jason muttered. Joshua nodded. But Jeremy had seen the truth in what the young woman had said.

"No, sh-she's right," he stated.

"What do you mean, she's right?" Joshua asked. "There's no razzle dazzle in that handbill. Not one word."

"Not in the h-handbill. But the way you t-t-talked."

"You just leave the talkin' to us. We'll make out all right, boy."

"No, you don't und-der-st-st..." Jeremy struggled hard with the words but just couldn't make them go. Hurt, he walked away from his brothers, dejected. Jason sighed and came up behind him.

"Jeremy! Now, Jeremy, just say what's on your mind," he said, sitting on the engine.

"I can't t-t-talk and you know it," Jeremy replied, his back still turned.

"Go ahead, Jeremy, just say it," Jason encouraged.

"All right," Jeremy said and with a deep breath, he turned to look at his kin. "These g-girls aren't the kind you're used to. They're not the Fr-Frisco kind. They're the kind Lottie s-s-said we should look for. They're honest, and they're ser-ser-serious."

"Girls are all the same," Joshua commented.

"No, they're not!" Jeremy's blue eyes blazed with anger now. "You're not askin' 'em to g-g-go upstairs for an hour. You're askin' 'em to go cl-clear across the country. To be away from their homes and f-families for the rest of their lives!"

"Well, Jeremy," Jason said thoughtfully, "what do *you* think we ought to do about it?"

"Well, when you-when you get up there on that pl-platform tonight, t-talk honest."

"All right, suppose you do," Joshua spoke to Jason. "What are you gonna say?"

"I don't know. I never talked honest to a girl a day in my life," Jason admitted as he linked his arms across his chest.

"There. You see? He wouldn't be able to open his mouth. Me neither." At Joshua's words, Jeremy turned away from them again. Jason reached out and put a hand on his shoulder.

"Now, now, Jeremy. Don't get scared. What about you? Why don't you talk to 'em?" he asked.

"Me?" Jeremy asked, panicked. "Oh no, please, n-not me, I c-can't, oh—"

"Then I guess we do it the old way, me and Jason together," Joshua said, expecting the argument to end.

"No!" Jeremy yelled. "I call for a f-family vote!"

"All right, family vote," Jason said. "Josh?"

"I vote for me and you together," he replied, shrugging. "Jeremy?"

"I v-v-vote Jason, by himself, t-t-talkin' honest."

"I vote," Jason began. He sighed and surprised even himself with his answer, "talkin' by myself and honest." Jeremy's face lit up in a smile, surprised. Joshua, on the other hand, was not so pleased.

"Ah, Jason. What are you gonna do? What are you gonna say?"

"Well, I'll talk the way Jeremy would," he replied, standing. He put an arm around Jeremy and smiled. "And if I can say it half as well as he can, I don't care if *I* stutter!" Joshua just shook his head and followed his brothers out.

The New Bedford City Hall was full to overflowing with women that evening. Some came with genuine interest, others were only curious. And then there was the young firefighter, Candy Pruitt. She turned out to be a very important person in the community, Jason found out, much to his chagrin. She would be a hard sell. But if Jason could win her over, the only problem would be deciding on who *couldn't* go.

Jeremy and Joshua each stood one step down, on either side of the platform. The room grew suddenly still as Jason took his place behind the podium. He took a few moments to look out over his audience. For perhaps the first time in his life, Jason Bolt was nervous. He looked at both his brothers then turned his full attention to the women.

"Now I want you all to know, and I'm talkin' to you honest, ladies and gentlemen—ah, ladies," he grinned as he paused, "that we'll sign a contract, same as you will, and we'll marry you." He paused again and laughed. "We'll find a fella for you to marry. And if you'll sign on and say you're marriageable…ah, you know what that means…"

"No, Mr. Bolt," Candy said, standing up. Jason drew a blank and he almost paled as Candy sat back down. Jason paced back and forth in front of the podium a moment. This wasn't going as well as he'd expected.

"Well, then, I'll be right up here if there are any questions," he said and went around behind the podium again.

"You bet there are, Mr. Bolt," Candy stated, standing once more. "Who are you? You and your brothers? Where are you taking us? Where is Seattle, anyway?"

"Washington Territory," Jason replied. He pulled out a

small, leather-bound booklet from a pocket inside his jacket and read. "Seattle…it's on the Puget Sound…population, 152, mostly men," he paused for effect and got it. The women quietly giggled. Jason went on to relate weather conditions—false conditions, but he decided the women would never know.

"That's fine, Mr. Bolt, you've got weather," Candy said, impatience coloring her tone. "So've we. What we're getting at," she looked around at the other women who nodded, "what about the men? Are they honest? Can a woman rely on them?"

"Are they good-lookin'?" Biddie Cloom asked.

"Are they tall?" another woman asked.

"Are they as tall as you?" came another question.

"Tall, lady?" Jason asked, smiling. He was finally back in control of the situation. He crossed over to where Jeremy stood and went on. "Why, where I come from, they call me…"

"Li'l half-pint," Jeremy whispered.

"Little half-pint," Jason stated, which got an approving nod from Joshua.

"Are they strong, Mr. Bolt? 'Cause I want a strong one," another lady questioned.

"Strong, sister? Why, when a Seattle man spits into the wind, tall trees fall down. And talk about trees. They punch holes right through the ceilin' of the sky." Jason moved closer to his audience, who appeared mesmerized by his descriptive phrasing. Jeremy's face brightened into a smile, then he and Candy exchanged shy glances. Jason continued in his persuasive, eloquent manner.

"Now, let me tell you about snow. You've never seen snow till you've seen it snow in Seattle. And the rain. Why, if you get wet in Seattle spring rain, you don't want to take a bath for a month 'cause you don't want to wash off how clean you feel." Jason's hands automatically gestured as he spoke. The women's faces seemed locked in a dreamlike state. "But the big thing, ladies…let me tell you about the big thing.

"I'll bet you think you know what the color green is. Evergreen, that's what it is. Green…like the mornin' the world started. Green...like the carpet of Adam and Eve. Green...like the mornin' the Lord first painted his garden. Green, forever green." He went behind the podium as he let his words sink in.

"Yes sir, ladies, we've got everything in Seattle, everything. But...we haven't got you. And, if we haven't got you, we haven't got anything." Jason paused and leaned over the podium. "So, who'll go?" The ladies hesitated and looked to Candy to make the first move. She looked around, nervously biting her lip. The looks on the others' faces told her what she knew she wanted, too. With a determined smile and a nod of her head, she stood up.

"I'll go!" she declared. The women rushed forward to sign the Bolt brothers' contract. Joshua and Jeremy barely had time to produce writing instruments.

That night, one hundred women signed on to journey to the wilderness of the Northwest. They signed on to the hope of a new life and fulfillment of their fondest dreams of having husbands, children, and homes they could call their own.

Chapter Six

Ben Perkins, owner of Seattle's General Store, stood away from the burning building. He and several others had been trying to save it but now, as evening approached, he knew the battle was lost. Ben had been one of Seattle's first citizens and his store had been one of the first permanent structures erected.

"Thanks, guys!" he shouted to the other men but disappointment colored his tone. "Thanks for trying!"

"Fire's gettin' too far spread, Ben," one of the firefighters stated. "Feel like helpin' with the rest?"

"Of course. I'm gonna go to the relief tent, first, get word to Em. See you in a bit." As the others gathered up their shovels, picks, and buckets, Ben wearily made his way toward where all the tents were pitched. It would be hard to tell his wife, Emily. Starting over would be hard after more than fourty years had gone by, but he knew Emily would be right there with Ben to do just that.

Inside the hospital tent, two doctors calmly saw to the treatment and comfort of their few patients. Doctors Sam Michaels and Allyn Wright worked quietly, thankful that the injuries had been minor ones.

"It's a miracle no one has been killed," Wright commented, her brown eyes deepening into a smile.

"You're not wrong there, Allyn," Michaels replied, a smile crinkling his weathered features. "But...it's far from over. Deputy Fire Chief Brandeis sent word that we can expect more casualties."

"The possibility of fatalities is high, isn't it?" Allyn asked quietly, not really expecting a reply. She'd been a part of Seattle for just over twenty years, and in that time, she'd seen radical changes. Not just in the city's growth, but in the people. Being a woman doctor, she'd expected most of the obstacles thrown in her way. And the people of Seattle had thrown her quite a few, but slowly, they'd adjusted to one another. Allyn smiled as she recalled the day Jason Bolt had brought her from San Francisco to Seattle.

"Dr. Wright!" one of the nurses shouted, breaking Allyn out of her reverie. She looked up to see Jason being aided by another man. Jason protested that he was all right, but Dr. Wright shut him up.

"You just sit here, Jason Bolt!" she commanded. "Got too close to the fire, I see." She gently examined his face and arms which showed that Jason *did* get too close. He sighed as he resigned himself to her expert care. "Well, only minor burns, but they'll need to be cleaned and treated. And I want you to stay here for a little while...get some rest."

"But, but—" Jason began.

"No buts, Jason! What I say goes around here. Understood?" Allyn smiled in spite of her authoritative tone.

"Understood, Doctor," Jason replied, defeated. As the

doctor gingerly cleaned the burns, Jason looked around the almost empty tent. "Looks like business is slow."

"Thank God for that. Most of the casualties have been like yours—minor burns and smoke inhalation. How far has the fire spread?"

"Almost half the waterfront businesses are gone. Ben Perkins lost his, too."

"Oh no, poor Emily. She and Ben worked so hard to keep it going."

"Yeah," Jason said sadly. Allyn applied a salve then bandaged only a couple of the wounds as Jason went on. "I'm afraid a lot more businesses are going to suffer as well. This fire is very hot, and I'm not trying to joke. Whatever caused this fire had to be just red-hot to start with to create such a fast spreading blaze in such a short amount of time."

"Any idea how it was set?"

"Not really, no. A few of us have a theory, but it'd be hard to prove at this point. All we can do is what's already being done—fight the spread."

Allyn started to say something else when Joshua came walking over. He heaved a sigh of relief as Jason smiled his way.

"Jason! Are you all right? What happened?" he asked.

"I'm all right," Jason assured him. "Just some minor burns. I got a little close. Where's Jeremy?"

"He's with one of the crews at the courthouse. I saw a man with a torch behind it and Jeremy and I tried to find him, but the courthouse burst into flames.

"Jeremy saw Douglas but we didn't have time to try and look for him. The firebreak Brandeis tried didn't work, so we've been trying to keep it contained by the courthouse."

"Sounds like Douglas may be a good suspect, huh?"

"Yeah, looks like. You know, it makes sense, too. I mean, he shows up at the wedding, accuses Kathryn of improper behavior, then ducks out before he can answer any questions."

"Well, I think you ought to let Jeremy handle this situation with Douglas," Wright interjected. "Kathryn is *his* daughter."

"Yeah, well, she's our niece and Jeremy's our brother," Joshua replied. "And we'll do anything we can to help him. Besides, Douglas was armed."

"That certainly puts matters in a different light," Jason said. "You see Jeremy, you tell him to be careful. I know you'll be there to help, Josh."

"Now then, I think it's time for Jason to get some rest," Allyn stated.

"All right. I'll check on you later, Jason."

"I think you should stop by the relief tent and let your wife know you're all right, Joshua," she said.

"Right, Doc," Joshua said with a grin. "Something cold to drink would taste good about now, too." He nodded to his brother then left. Jason lay back and closed his eyes. His burns didn't really hurt all that much, but he was tired.

Joshua walked inside the tent, spotted his wife, and headed toward her. He nodded to Candy but startled Callie as he came up behind her.

"How about something cold to drink, ladies?" he asked cheerfully.

"Josh! Oh, Joshua! Are you all right?" Callie asked as she hugged her husband.

"I'm all right, don't worry," he replied with a grin. As Callie adjusted her glasses, Joshua turned to his sister-in-law. "Jeremy's fine, too, Candy."

"Thank you," she said, sighing.

"Listen, can you fill up about ten canteens with water?" Joshua asked. "I'm heading back to where Jeremy is. I know the men would welcome a cool drink!"

"Of course," Callie said, taking the canteens from her husband. "This fire isn't slowing down, is it?" She and Candy quickly filled the canteens.

"No, not at all. Jason was hurt," Joshua said, then quickly added, "He's gonna be all right. Dr. Wright says he just got some minor burns and he's resting now."

"Josh, have you seen Clancey?" Candy asked.

"Not for a while. He said something about checking on his ol' tub."

"The fire isn't threatening the harbor, is it?" Callie asked.

"No, not yet anyway. But I'll send someone to check on Clancey. Well, better head on back. I'll tell Jeremy I saw you, Candy." Candy nodded, smiling. She went back to the buffet line as other men came in on break. Callie and Joshua exchanged a brief hug then he left.

Captain Roland Francis Clancey was trying to pack some of his treasured belongings into a box. Every now and then, he wiped a tear from his weathered face. He knew he could lose his ship. The fire was getting very close. The *Shamus O'Flynn* wasn't much of a ship compared with the newer ones sitting in the harbor, but she was Clancey's. He'd sailed her for going on fifty years and he didn't know if he could bear losing her.

The fire was about to get a lot closer. A man, poorly dressed, came swaggering toward the fishing boats. He carried a cold torch in one hand and a bottle of cheap booze in the other. Guzzling a drink now and then, he slowly got closer to the boats. Laughing, he set his bottle down, then lit the torch. He paused momentarily, seemingly lost in thought, then awkwardly tossed the torch onto the deck of one of the smaller boats. Hooting with laughter, he picked up his bottle and staggered away from the dock. Startled by the sudden appearance of other men, the drunkard dropped his bottle and paper bag and began to run. Some of the men ran after him, while others stayed behind to put out the fire.

The fleeing man managed to elude his pursuers and the chase ended abruptly. As they headed back toward the docks, the unkempt man hid behind some Chinese workers in an alley. As soon as it appeared safe, he laughed, albeit uneasily, and headed on up the alley.

Firefighters worked at extinguishing the flames on the fishing boats. The main fire was spreading ever closer to the docks and some of the other ships were now in danger of burning. To prevent that, some of the ship owners were busily trying to get their boats out into the open water of the bay. Clancey's ship was anchored close to the fishing fleet but none of the firefighters knew the old sea captain was still on board.

Joshua and Jeremy Bolt ran up just then and started for the *Shamus O'Flynn*. One of the firefighters stopped them from getting too close to the ships.

"Have you seen Capt. Clancey?" Joshua asked loudly.

"No. Haven't seen anyone since we chased a bum out of here. We think he's the one setting the fires," the man stated.

"Where is he?" Jeremy asked.

"Lost him. We chased him as far as the Chinese district and it was like he just vanished. Anyway, he set the boats on fire so we came back to help with that."

"Well, we've got to go on board Clancey's boat. He could still be there," Joshua said.

"Your necks!" the firefighter said with a shrug. "His boat's awfully close to the fire."

"Yeah," Jeremy muttered. The two brothers quickly resumed their way toward Clancey's old scow. Flames leapt out at them, threatening to engulf the ship at any moment. With quick glances to one another, the men jumped aboard the ship.

"Clancey! Clancey, you here?" Joshua yelled.

"Check his cabin, Josh!" Without another word, they went below deck to the only real cabin on the whole boat. Clancey was startled as they came busting inside. Though puzzled by their looks of relief, he smiled.

"Ah, two of me pals! But yas look like hell," he said.

"Come on, Clancey," Joshua said, taking Clancey by the arm. "We gotta get out of here. The fire is *very* close."

"I know. I've been packin' some of me old t'ings."

"All right, Clancey," Jeremy said, picking up a box. "I've got your stuff. Let's go." Clancey sadly looked around the sparse cabin.

"All right, lads, right behind yas." He quickly followed Joshua and Jeremy out the open cabin door.

As they quietly watched the firefighters battle the flames, Clancey's face streaked with tears. He would never see his ship again.

"Clancey, we'll stay and help," Jeremy said softly and put a hand on the old man's arm. "We'll do everything we can to save her, you know that."

"Aye, I know." The Bolt brothers had seen Clancey depressed before, but losing his ship would be tough on him.

"Look, Clancey, you could do us a favor," Joshua began. "Jason got some burns...he's okay, but we'd appreciate it if you could go to the hospital tent and check on him."

"All right, Joshua. You're good lads!" The old captain surprised the brothers as he gave them both hugs, then took his box from Jeremy and left. Joshua and Jeremy exchanged grins then set about helping combat the spreading fire.

Chapter Seven

By late evening, flames still engulfed the waterfront buildings. Men worked in shifts to battle the blaze but they seemed to be losing the war. Water pressure suddenly dropped and the firefighters started shouting commands at the others.

"Get buckets!" Brandeis shouted. "Start hauling water from the bay!" A short, squat figure of man, the fire chief spoke with a voice that belied his size. And when he barked, the men didn't ask questions.

This night was no different. Some of the men paired off to retrieve more containers while others headed for the bay with the buckets already on hand. A sense of panic hung over the men, but they worked nonstop.

Just north of town, men were just about finished covering

Aaron Stempel's house with wet blankets. Stempel had been hard at work all day, it seemed. He could feel the heat from the threatening fire and continued at a fevered pace. He was determined to save his house. At least his sawmill was too far away to be at risk.

"We gotta have more help at the fire!" a man yelled as he rushed up to the sawmill owner. "Water pressure's gone! We gotta haul water up from the bay!" At that, almost everyone left.

"Thought you might need some help!" Jason Bolt shouted. He immediately began helping Stempel toss the last of the blankets onto the house.

"Thanks! How'd you get away from the good doctor?" Stempel asked.

"Just told her I was all right," Jason stated with a shrug. Their task completed, the two men backed away from the house. It was an odd-looking structure now.

"Now we wait!" Stempel shouted.

"Yeah, yeah," Jason said, nodding. "I think it'll work, Aaron."

"Let's hope you're right."

"How about some coffee?"

"Nah. I think I'll stay awhile. Thanks, Jason." Jason nodded and patted Stempel on the back, then headed up the hill toward the relief tent. His long nap had refreshed him and now he was hungry.

Around midnight, Jeremy joined Joshua in front of the Seattle Hotel. The fire had not spread to the ornate structure as of yet, and the two men looked the building over. The hotel was one of the finest in the territory and they would do all they could to save it.

"Looks like we better get a crew here pretty soon," Joshua stated.

"Looks like," Jeremy agreed. "Listen, Josh, why don't you go get some sleep? I managed to get a couple of hours earlier. Just send me a crew down here first."

"Sounds like a plan. You gonna be all right here?"

"Sure. I'll poke around a little, try to judge the best places to shore up. Or figure out what things to try and save. Just make sure a crew gets here as soon as possible. I don't think Brandeis is gonna be able to keep the fire out of here completely."

"Yeah, I know. You know, once this is all over, Aaron Stempel is going to have some explaining to do."

"Why's that?" Jeremy asked, puzzled.

"Because of the water pressure dropping. He was in charge of the project, you know. There's already talk goin' around that he took shortcuts because of the cost involved with a new water line."

"Oh. We'll just have to see, I guess. You better get going."

"Yeah." Joshua hesitated then turned back to his brother. "Jeremy, why don't you come back with me? You can take the—"

"Josh, you sound like Candy!" Jeremy interrupted with a chuckle. "I'm just fine here. I'm a big boy!"

"I know that, but I feel uneasy about you being here alone."

"Josh, if the fire gets too close, I'll get out."

"Will you?" Joshua asked, unsure. "You know how you get—"

"I think I know how to make intelligent decisions, Joshua." Jeremy's tone took on an edge as his temper threatened to flare. He knew his brother was concerned, but sometimes Joshua pushed too far.

"I'm not questioning your ability, Jeremy," Joshua replied coolly. "You sometimes get pig-headed and you don't always watch out for your own safety!"

"Thank you for pointing out the flaws in my character, Brother! I think we'd both be better off if you'd leave, right now." Both brothers sized one another up mentally but stood their ground. Suddenly, Joshua began laughing. "I don't see anything funny about—" Jeremy began but Joshua cut him off.

"We're acting like a couple of fools!" he stated, stifling his laughter.

"Yeah, I guess we are," Jeremy chuckled in agreement. He stuck out his hand. "Sorry, Josh."

"Likewise," Joshua replied, taking his brother's hand. "I'll send a crew down right away. But watch yourself, all right? I mean, if you saw Douglas once—"

"I'll watch out, don't worry."

"All right. I'll let Candy know you're okay."

"Thanks, Josh. Get some rest." Joshua clapped his brother on the back and left.

Jeremy lit a torch and went inside the hotel. It was already warm in the lobby and the fire wasn't all that close yet. Jeremy sighed as he looked around the grand old lady. It had been one of the first really fancy buildings in Seattle. The lobby was copied after one of the hotels in San Francisco—very ornate and spacious.

A sudden noise from somewhere above got Jeremy's immediate attention. It appeared to be coming from one of the rooms upstairs. Jeremy cautiously headed up the winding steps toward the sound, surprised that anyone would be in the hotel now. The entire downtown area had been evacuated hours before.

Joshua sat with Jason in the relief tent, having coffee though neither drank much. Jason finally got up and put his cup back, nodding to one of the ladies behind the table. When he turned back around, Joshua was heading toward the opening of the tent. It took Jason only a few strides to catch up.

"You got a crew out right away to the hotel?" he asked, knowing what was on his brother's mind.

"Yeah," Joshua sighed. "Corky, McGee, and some others were getting some things together to take over. Jeremy was just gonna look the place over. I'm sure he'll get out of there if it gets too dangerous."

"But—"

"Oh, we—Jeremy and me—almost came to blows." Joshua

looked up at Jason and shook his head. "Can you believe that? In the middle of all this hell, we still found time to fight!"

"About what?"

"Safety. I got a little overbearing, I guess, and Jeremy's temper got the better of both of us and we argued. Looking out for him is a hard habit to break."

"You're not the only one, Joshua," Candy stated as she joined her in-laws. "I didn't mean to eavesdrop."

"You're welcome anytime, Candy, you know that," Jason said.

"So, what were you saying about my stubborn husband?" she asked, smiling.

"Not hard to guess, huh?" Joshua asked, not expecting a reply. "I just worried about leaving him there alone. I mean, the fire is bad enough, but knowing that Jerome Douglas is out there somewhere, armed..." He paused when he saw Candy pale at the thought. "I'm sure Jeremy will watch out though. He's not stupid."

"And Corky and his crew should be there about now," Jason said.

"I know you're right. But that hotel is big and if Jeremy gets too busy poking around—"

"He's a smart man, Candy; he'll be careful," Jason said.

"Corky'll root him out of there!" Joshua laughed. Candy finally smiled and nodded. "Come on, I could use a drink!"

"Well, the strongest you'll get is lemonade!" Candy stated and walked back inside with the Bolts.

Jeremy cautiously walked down the long corridor of the hotel as the sounds continued. Armed with only a torch, he was beginning to wish he'd gone back with Joshua. At the very least, he should've kept a gun in his belt, but he'd left it at the relief tent earlier.

As he opened a door, two cats came flying out of the room, startling him, and he dropped his torch. He chuckled as he picked up the glowing light. Upon hearing only silence, Jeremy went back downstairs to the lobby.

Jeremy took his pocket watch out again, for about the third time. He couldn't understand why a crew hadn't gotten to the hotel yet. He knew Joshua would have stressed that they hurry. Jeremy grinned at that.

A shuffling noise caught his attention and he turned but saw nothing. He went and sat down on the cushiony lobby seat. It was plush and very comfortable, but it was too warm to worry about falling asleep. Jeremy sighed. If the crew didn't get there soon, he was going to go look for them.

The shuffling noise alerted his senses once more and he stood up. Again, he saw nothing and shook his head. His nerves were being tested. But the shuffling grew louder and Jeremy whirled around to see Jerome Douglas standing just inside the edge of the circle of light from the torch.

"I figured you'd show sooner or later," Jeremy said, anger welling up inside him. Douglas calmly lit one of the lobby's globe lamps. Jeremy noticed the holstered gun on Douglas but said nothing.

"You're unarmed, I see," the man said.

"I see no need to carry a gun," Jeremy replied quietly. "You have a lot of questions to answer."

"Yes, I know. I hear I'm being blamed for the fire as well."

"That thought has occurred to a lot of people."

"Including you?"

"I would be lying if I said it hadn't crossed my mind. It's a little farfetched, I must admit, to think that you would deliberately set fire to an entire city just because you're jealous."

"But?"

"But your earlier actions were unusual too."

"Point well made, Mr. Bolt," Douglas replied, pulling up a nearby stool. "However, I assure you that I did not start the fire."

"I don't see that your assurances count for much!"

"Ah, the offended father! I understand that young Mr. Fairfield isn't convinced that his fair maiden is...just that!"

"Why you son of a bitch!" Jeremy shouted angrily and

started forward but halted when Douglas rested his hand on his gun. Jeremy's blue eyes narrowed as he went on. "How dare you come into my daughter's life and accuse her of...of..."

"I believe the term you're looking for is improprieties! Can you say it, Mr. Bolt? Or does it stick in your throat?" Jeremy remained silent for the moment, seething with inner rage. Douglas slowly stood and unholstered his weapon. "Your 'little' girl isn't, Mr. Bolt. Wide-eyed, innocent girls are so easily persuaded by older men!"

"What...what exactly did my daughter...did she do with you?" Jeremy asked, trying to maintain a calm demeanor. It would do no good to goad Douglas into a reason to use his gun.

"What didn't she do is more to the point," Douglas laughed.

"Very well. I'd like to know specifics," Jeremy said, sitting back down.

"I'm surprised you haven't asked her."

"I have. She admits she met you...knew about you. But she was never alone with you. Not-Not like you've implied. Now, if my daughter has lied to me, I'd like to know."

"Perhaps we should wait until Kathryn can be here as well." Jeremy reacted without thinking and stood up, shouting.

"Damn it! Kathryn has been involved in this all she's gonna! I don't think you can answer the question because there's nothing to say. You've been lying all along. I wasn't sure before about why, but I believe now that you are jealous. And I am sure that you're out to make my daughter's life miserable!"

"Calling me a liar is a pretty dangerous thing, Mr. Bolt. Especially when I'm the one armed!" Douglas stood as well; his dark eyes narrowed.

"Shooting me won't get you anywhere," Jeremy said quietly, swallowing hard as he suddenly realized the corner he'd painted Douglas into. "There's a crew on its way here right now."

"No, Mr. Bolt, they won't be here for quite some time. You

see, they were given a different location. Seems you changed your mind about the hotel being in danger after all."

"You can shoot me…kill me, Douglas, but you'll never get away with it. My f-family will hunt you down." Jeremy's voice was firm and calm, but sweat moistened his face just the same.

"I'd be nervous, too!" Douglas laughed then stopped as he heard noises outside. "Sounds like the fire is catching up to us."

"Sounds that way. Why don't you holster your gun and we'll talk to Kathryn."

"You really don't get it, do you? You think I'm just gonna go quietly? Didn't Kathryn tell you how dangerous I am?"

"She said she'd heard some things about you," Jeremy said slowly, trying to stall for time as the noises outside grew closer, "but she didn't know if they were true."

"You're a very bad liar, Mr. Bolt," Douglas replied, edgy. "But don't worry, I'll tell Kat what a good father she has…had!"

Ignoring the threat to his life, Jeremy replied heatedly, "You touch my daughter and—"

"And what? And nothing! You'll be dead!" Douglas practically spat out his words. As the noises outside grew louder still, Douglas turned his attention away from Jeremy for just a moment. Jeremy seized the opportunity and began backing up, trying to make it into the shadows. But his efforts were in vain. Douglas turned and quickly fired twice. Jeremy fell backward as the punishing bullets struck him hard in the upper body. As he hit the floor, the force of the impact rolled him over. Then, everything was still. Douglas started for Jeremy to make sure he was dead but decided to make a hasty exit instead. He could see that the fire was well on its way to including the hotel. If the bullets hadn't killed Jeremy Bolt, the fire would take care of him.

As soon as Douglas was gone, Jeremy slowly rolled onto his back. Douglas' shots, while somewhat off target, still found human flesh to zero in on. The front of Jeremy's shirt was already saturated with blood. Jeremy grunted as he tried to get up, but the fiery pain in his chest forced him back to the floor. Breathing heavily, he slowly ran his tongue over his lips. As perspiration rolled down his face, Jeremy tried to assess how badly injured he was.

He found it next to impossible to move his right arm, so he knew he'd caught a bullet near his shoulder. He bit down on his lip as the fingers of his left hand let him know where the other bullet had struck—the middle of his chest. He figured he couldn't have been hit in the heart, since he was still alive.

"Oh God...please..." he whispered. The pain kept him from saying anything else but he heard shouting from somewhere outside. At that moment glass shattered somewhere in the hotel. Jeremy knew then that the fire had surely hit and he knew he had to get out.

Anticipating the pain from his wounds, Jeremy inched his feet up and pushed himself toward the front entrance. He didn't stop to think about how many steps there were. Just making it over to the first step would be an accomplishment. Gasping with every move, he made the agonizing slide over. He closed his eyes for a moment and swallowed. Through blurred vision, he looked up at what seemed to be an insurmountable climb. Gritting his teeth, he tried to roll up onto the step but the effort sent new waves of pain crashing over him.

He tried desperately to hang on to consciousness; he told himself someone surely would have heard the gunshots. But as his body slid back to the lobby floor, Jeremy felt a sense of panic and relief at the same time. A burning pain stabbed at his chest. With an anguished cry, he sank into painless blackness.

Chapter Eight

"Clancey, are ya sure you want to go down there? It's so late," Jason asked as he and the old sea dog trudged down the hill from the relief tent.

"Aye, I am, bucko," Clancey replied sadly. "If me ship's goin' down, I want to say a proper good-bye."

"You know, we may not be able to get that close."

"I hear yas, Jason." The two men walked the rest of the way in silence. They found a long line of smoldering remnants that had once been buildings...businesses owned by friends. Jason heaved a deep sigh and sadness was the only light mirrored in his blue eyes as they walked past.

"Evenin', Jason, Capt.," a worker called out to the two men as they carefully made their way toward the harbor.

"Jamison," Jason acknowledged. Jamison went on about

his work, removing debris.

Jason and Clancey arrived at the berths just in time to see the mast of the *Shamus O'Flynn* slowly disappear under the murky waters of Elliot Bay. Everywhere else, clouds of dark smoke made an already dark night that much blacker. Jason put a gentle hand on Clancey's shoulder, knowing there was absolutely nothing he could say to comfort the man. They stood there for a few minutes, each man lost in his own thoughts.

"Come on, Clancey," Jason finally said. "There's nothing more to be done here."

"Ah Jason, she's gone," Clancey sobbed mournfully. "Me life's gone! Fifty years I sailed her and not once did she complain."

"I know, I know. Please, Clancey. Come stay at my house, all right?"

"Aye, bucko, aye." The captain dragged a weary hand across his tear-streaked face, nodding.

What will he do now? Jason thought. *What can he do?*

"I could use a drink," Jason said. Perhaps he could get a few shots down Clancey as well. "A good, stiff one." Clancey only nodded and turned his back on half a century of his own history.

Corky Masters, McGee, and three other men slowly picked their way toward the Seattle Hotel. Joshua Bolt had been urgent with his request for them to meet up with Jeremy. A messenger, supposedly sent by Jeremy, had caught up to the crew just as they had come within sight of the majestic building. The man's message had made sense to Corky; the hotel really wasn't in any immediate danger but the old opera house was. And so, the crew had headed away from the hotel, unknowingly endangering Jeremy's life.

Now, as they drew near to the hotel almost an hour later, Corky could see that the grand old building was indeed in danger. He shook his head. *Boy, is Jeremy gonna be mad at me!*

"What do you think, Corky?" McGee asked as the men stopped in front of the building. It was such a massive structure that, even though fire was belching out of one of the upper floors, it was still far from being destroyed.

"Guess we do what we can. And keep an eye out for Jeremy Bolt," Corky replied.

"If he's still around here, he's gonna be pretty sore it took us so long to get here."

"Yeah, well, we've got a bigger problem to worry about right now. Besides, how were we to know that message was a phony? I'm gonna take a couple of guys inside and see if we can save anything."

"I'll send Samuels for more help," McGee offered and Corky nodded in agreement. As he and two other men went up the marble steps toward the entrance, McGee sent Samuels for a bigger crew.

Corky quickly kicked the door in, afraid that flames would leap out at them from beyond. The entrance was free of fire for the moment, however, and Corky went in first. There were four steps to ascend upon entering, then six steps down into the lobby. The lamp Douglas had lit earlier was barely glowing, and the torch Jeremy'd had was completely out. Corky narrowed his eyes as he peered into the shadows.

"Well, there's some light," he said then turned to his men. "All right, real easy here. Forbes, you check out the upstairs. Rollins, check out the parlor area. I'll see what I can do about…" He paused when he spotted a body at the bottom of the steps. "Wait!" he shouted to the others. In two jumps, he was at Jeremy's side. "Come down here! It's Jeremy!" he yelled. He turned Jeremy over and felt for a pulse. Upon finding one, Corky heaved a sigh of relief.

"He alive?" Forbes asked.

"Barely. C'mon, help me get him out of here." The three men lifted Jeremy's limp form and quickly carried him outside. Corky spotted a group of men with a litter and quickly shouted for their help. They put Jeremy onto the canvas carrier and rushed him to the hospital tent.

Corky arrived several steps ahead of the others and ran inside. Upon seeing Dr. Michaels nearby, Corky grabbed the older man by the arm.

"Come quick, Doc!" Corky was almost breathless. "It's Jeremy Bolt! He's been hurt real bad!"

"All right, lay him down over here!" Michaels shouted as the men ran in with the litter. The doctor helped them carefully slide Jeremy onto the examination table. "What happened?" Michaels asked as he began his examination.

"Don't know for sure," Corky replied, twisting his hat in his hands. "All I know is we went to the hotel and found Jeremy lying unconscious inside. He'll be all right, won't he, Doc?" But the doctor didn't answer right away as he quickly removed Jeremy's shirt. Gritting his teeth, Michaels finally looked back up at Corky, a grim look on his face.

"He's been shot...twice," he said quietly.

"Shot?" Corky asked, dumbfounded.

"Yeah. It looks bad, Corky. You better get the Bolts."

"He ain't..."

"No, not yet. Now hurry!" Corky nodded and ran out of the tent. Michaels immediately yelled at one of the nurses to assist him. "We've got gunshot wounds here, Ann! I'll need as much ether as you can find."

"Morphine?" Ann asked.

"Yes. I hope we'll need it later. Now please hurry." The young nurse nodded and quickly retrieved the requested items, then returned to the doctor's side. Michaels looked up at her and drew in a deep breath. "Never expected to see this," he muttered. "Fire's bad enough but..." he didn't finish as he began probing for the bullets he knew were imbedded in his patient.

Candy handed Jason a cup of coffee, then sat down next to him. She was tired, sad, and worried. As she watched the glowing scene far below from where she was, she knew her husband was in all that chaos somewhere. A sudden chill caught her by surprise and she shivered.

"Cold?" Jason asked quietly.

"Just got a chill. I'm all right," she replied. "It's so hard to see it go like this."

"Yes. Yes, it is." Jason's brow furrowed together and he sighed. "I hope Jeremy got enough sleep earlier."

"Catnapped mostly. You know how he is!" They both managed a chuckle at that.

"I'm glad Josh finally got some rest. I feel selfish."

"Well, you did stray a little close, now, didn't you?" Candy teased. "That's what you get for playing with fire." She laughed and Jason only shook his head.

"I suppose—"

"Jason! Jason!" Corky Masters interrupted as he reached the eldest Bolt brother. He took only a second to catch his breath. "It's Jeremy! He's been hurt. He—"

"Hurt?" Candy asked, feeling chilled again. "How bad? Where is he?"

"It's real bad, Candy." Corky turned to face Jason again. "Jason, he was shot!"

"Hospital tent?" Jason asked, frowning.

"Yeah. The doc's working on him now. We got him to the hospital as quick as we could, Jason." Corky looked directly at Candy and added, "I'm sorry, Candy."

"Oh no, dear God," she whispered as tears automatically spilled down her face. Jason quickly took her by the arm.

"Let's get over there. We can't find out anything standing here. Corky, see if you can find Josh." Corky nodded as he patted Candy's arm, then ran down the hill. Candy was silent as she allowed her brother-in-law to lead her over to the hospital tent, just a short distance away.

As they entered, a nurse led them to a couple of waiting chairs. Candy's eyes wandered around the tent until she spotted a curtained-off area. That was where Jeremy was, she knew. She bit down on her lip as Ann Matthews came toward them.

"It's going to be awhile," the nurse said softly. "Jeremy was shot twice, in the chest. Dr. Michaels says there's no damage to the heart. But..."

"But it's real bad, isn't it?" Candy asked, her chin quivering. "Corky said..." but she couldn't finish as tears continued to roll down her cheeks. Jason took her hand and turned to Ann.

"We'll be right here, Ann. Thanks for coming over," he said.

Ann hurried back to the operating area. Another nurse assisted Dr. Michaels, handing him instruments as he requested them. Ann monitored Jeremy's pulse and breathing. The doctor looked up momentarily as he placed the first bullet into a metal container.

"How's he doing, Ann?" he asked as he carefully checked for any bleeders before beginning to look for the second projectile.

"Weak. His breathing is very shallow," she replied. "Jason and Candy are waiting."

"All right. I only hope..." his thought didn't need to be finished, and he continued with his grisly task. "This one didn't go in as deep, at least. Traveled high into his shoulder and right out."

"His arm was really dangling when they brought him in," Ann began as she placed a couple more drops of ether onto the cloth that covered Jeremy's nose and mouth.

"Well, doesn't appear to be all that much damage to any nerves," Michaels replied. "Use of his arm's gonna be the least of his worries for quite a while." Nothing more was said for some time as they fervently worked into the early morning hours.

Meanwhile, Joshua had gone to the Seattle Opera House to try and help but it was too late. Once the hot flames had hit, the old theatre was doomed. Joshua stood back with the fire chief and other workers as they helplessly watched the roof cave in at last. They stared in stunned silence as much of downtown Seattle blazed not far from where they stood. The fire chief knew all they could do now was keep it from spreading any farther; it was a fire out of control.

"Well, at least it's headed for the water!" Joshua yelled over the noise of the inferno.

"Yeah!" Brandeis shouted, nodding. "That should stop it! Come on, we can't do any more here!" Joshua nodded and his attention was drawn to Corky Masters, who was running their way. Joshua waited for Corky to catch up.

"Josh! Get to the hospital tent now! Jeremy's been shot!" Corky yelled as he came to a halt in front of the middle brother. Shock registered on Joshua's dirt-streaked face, but he didn't ask questions. He just jumped on the nearest horse and was off. Corky remained with the others and sadly shook his head.

Chapter Nine

As dawn broke, Aaron Stempel watched with misty, weary eyes as the fire slowly burned itself out. Most of the hot flames had been extinguished and the smoke wasn't nearly as dense it had been. Men's soot-covered faces told the story as they continued to clear away debris.

Stempel heaved a sigh and headed for his house. His hard efforts had paid off for him at least. His house had survived. He decided it was time to get some real sleep at last. He'd catnapped, like most of the rest, but he'd been reminded several times that he was not a spring chicken. And he'd had to agree and let the younger men tackle the heart of the fire.

Inside the hospital tent, the fire was far from the minds of the Bolt family. Jeremy had been in surgery for hours it seemed, but they quietly waited. There were no words to speak…nothing anyone could say that would ease the anxiety.

Michaels heaved a weary sigh as he removed his bloodstained coveralls. He gave his sleeping patient a brief look-over before going out to speak with the family. Jeremy was pale despite having a mild fever. The doctor nodded to a nurse then pushed the drapes aside and went out.

"Jason," Candy whispered when she saw Michaels come out. She, Jason, and Joshua all stood up as the doctor approached. But he sat down and nodded, and everyone else sat down again.

"I won't lie to you about Jeremy's chances," he said honestly.

"Which are?" Jason asked.

"They could be better." He paused and looked into each face before going on. "He was shot twice in the chest. One wound is quite deep. But no damage to his heart…he's very lucky in that respect. One of the bullets went out through his right shoulder and he'll have restrictive movement for a while, but no paralysis."

"It's just going to take some time. He lost a lot of blood."

"Well, if you need donors, you just ask," Joshua stated, his chin quivering.

"Don't worry, I will," the doctor said gently and even smiled. "I know I can count on you."

"May I…see him?" Candy asked softly.

"Of course. Come with me." Michaels led them all to the area of the tent that had been curtained off. One by one, the family quietly followed the doctor inside. A nurse was placing a compress to Jeremy's forehead as they entered. He was still unconscious. Candy gently touched her husband's hand.

"He'll sleep quite a while," Michaels said softly. "We'll really know more about his chances once he's conscious."

"I want to stay with him," Candy said firmly. Michaels started to protest but Jason put up a hand, shaking his head. The doctor finally nodded defeatedly. Then another thought occurred to him.

"All right, Candy. At least your staying with him will free

up my nurses. There are plenty of compresses but if you run out, let us know. The fever is normal but it needs to be broken." He patted Candy's shoulder as she pulled up a chair. She would keep vigil over the man she loved.

"We'll take turns, Candy," Joshua said. "It won't do for any one of us to stay too long."

"All right, Josh," she agreed with a sigh. "I know you're right. But I will stay with him first. Do me a favor, please?"

"Name it."

"Get Kathryn and Jonathan. Have them come here?"

"You bet." Candy nodded and Joshua quickly left.

"If he wakes up, get me or Dr. Wright. She'll be here in a couple of hours," Michaels instructed Candy.

"I'll do that. Thank you."

"We'll do all we can to pull him through. You know that," the doctor stated.

"I know."

"Come on, Jason. I want to look at your burns," Michaels said.

"I'm all…," Jason protested then looked up at the doctor and grinned. "Coming. I'll be right outside, Candy." His sister-in-law managed a small smile for him, then he left with the doctor.

Joshua and Callie stood on the front porch of Jeremy's house, respectful of Candy's wishes yet uncertain about how to tell Jeremy's children about his condition. Callie placed a gentle hand on her husband's arm and nodded. Joshua opened the door and they stepped inside. To their surprise, Kathryn was already up and their sudden presence startled her.

"What's wrong?" she asked as she stood, seemingly frozen to the spot. Her soft blue eyes reflected fear more than worry.

"Let's go sit down," Callie offered.

"It's Daddy, isn't it?" She'd seen the sadness in her uncle's eyes.

"Yes," he replied and held out his arm to his niece.

Kathryn took it without another word and the three of them went into the drawing room. They sat down and Joshua took in a deep breath. "Jeremy was shot. No one knows for certain how it happened or exactly when. Sometime early this morning."

"Where?"

"At the hotel. I went to get some rest and Jeremy stayed to see what needed to be done. I sent Corky and a crew down right away. But someone told Corky that Jeremy had gone on to the opera house instead. Only he hadn't. And when the crew did get over to the hotel, Jeremy had already been...he'd been shot." Joshua paused and bit down on his lip.

"Is Daddy gonna be all right?" Kathryn asked tearfully.

"The doctor doesn't know yet," her uncle replied. "It's gonna be awhile yet."

"Once your father regains consciousness, the doctors will know more," Callie said, nervously rubbing her hands on her skirts, a habit she'd never outgrown.

"There's a chance he won't...he might not wake up, isn't there?" Kathryn began sobbing. Joshua leaned over and took her by the shoulders, forcing her to look him in the eye.

"No," he said firmly. "I don't believe that for a second. Your father's beat tough odds before. He'll beat this." His voice softened as he let go of his niece and she stood up. "He has to." Kathryn went over to look out at the sunrise. She smiled and turned back to her aunt and uncle.

"Daddy always liked a sunrise," she said.

"Yeah, he always was an early riser," Joshua stated and grinned.

"Any idea how this happened?" Kathryn's question took Joshua by surprise.

"I have a pretty strong idea," he replied.

"Jerome Douglas," Kathryn stated as if she should've thought of it sooner.

"I think so. We're going to search for him as soon as we can."

"I'd heard he could be ruthless, but I guess I never thought he'd go this far," Kathryn said quietly. "I tried to warn Daddy. But I had no idea…"

"No one could have, Kathryn," Joshua said. There was no point in telling her that Jeremy had seen Douglas prior to being hurt.

"Would you like me to wake up Jonathan?" Callie asked.

"No, no thanks," Kathryn said, sighing. "I'd better do it. I'll be back in a moment. Some coffee might help, though."

Callie nodded as she and Joshua headed for the kitchen while Kathryn went up the stairs to wake her little brother.

Chapter Ten

A man staggered drunkenly past a Chinese laundry, seemingly headed toward the waterfront. His tattered clothes and disheveled appearance gave away his status as one of Seattle's many homeless. Although there were jobs to be had, most were pretty menial and a lot of men refused to work for the meager wages. And unemployment was sure to escalate now in the aftermath of the fire.

The man went past people already hard at work and snickered. The Orientals were a strange bunch, he decided. They worked long hours for next to nothing. Not him though...not like that! The workers paid him no mind and he continued on his way, a paper bag in one hand and a half-empty bottle of whiskey in the other.

As he left the Chinese district, he carefully looked toward

downtown Seattle, or what was left of it, and laughed. Then, he swaggered on down to the waterfront where there didn't appear to be any danger of fire.

Brandeis and his men were hard at work as well, cleaning up the charred remains of the buildings along the main part of the city's waterfront. What had once been one of the most prosperous districts now lay in smoldering ruins.

One of the firefighters noticed a drunken man who seemed headed toward the edge of the water. He shook his head and looked for his boss.

"Hey, Chief! Look over there!" he called out.

"What is it, Marks?" Brandeis asked, looking up.

"See that bum over there?" Marks asked. Brandeis nodded. "Better go get him outta the way, huh?"

"Yeah," Brandeis sighed. "No sense letting him wander around down here. Poor soul."

"Jail's still standing," another firefighter stated.

"Nah," Marks said, laying his shovel aside, "the folks from the mission set a tent up by the others. I'll take him there." Marks walked toward the drunken man, who was busy talking to himself. He saw the firefighter coming his way and started to run. Marks shook his head but continued walking. He didn't see any reason to run; he knew he could outdistance the old man easily enough.

A sudden explosion ripped through a bank building as Marks got nearer to the man. Bricks flew all over as the building broke apart from the blast. Marks was hurled to the ground but the drunkard had gotten clear as if he'd known where to run to. The other firefighters rushed to the downed man.

Jason and Michaels sat quietly in the hospital tent. A woman had brought in some fresh coffee and pastries. Neither man opted to eat but did fill their cups with the strong brew. The doctor yawned and rolled his head around. It had been a long shift.

Allyn Wright entered the tent, a cheerful smile on her face, unaware of what had happened to Jeremy. One look at Jason Bolt's saddened face erased her smile.

"You're here early, Jason," she said as she put her medical bag down. "Is something wrong?"

"Jeremy was shot a few hours ago," Jason replied quietly. "Candy's with him right now, down there," he pointed to the curtained area.

"Shot?" Allyn asked, stunned. "But how…who?"

"We don't know anything for certain yet. Only speculation."

"Why don't you go on home, Sam?" she said to Michaels. "I'll take over."

"Thanks, I will. Send for me if you need me," he replied.

"Of course. I'll go see how Jeremy's doing."

"I'll come with you," Jason told her as he stood up. He faced Michaels and added, "Thanks for all you've done." Michaels nodded and patted Jason's arm. As he gathered up his things to leave, Allyn and Jason quietly walked through the tent.

Candy was folding dry compresses when Jason and Allyn entered. She shook her head at them in answer to their unspoken question. Allyn gently examined Jeremy, who appeared to be resting comfortably.

"Has his fever been very high?" she asked.

"I think so. He moans every now and then," Candy answered.

"Good. Maybe he'll come to soon. He's cool."

"Has the fever broken?" Jason asked, crossing his arms.

"For now," Wright said. "What happened, Jason?"

"Well, from what Corky told us, when he found Jeremy, he was already unconscious. Michaels said Jeremy had probably been like that for a little while. Exactly how long, no one knows."

"Well, his heartbeat's a bit fast," Allyn said as she removed her stethoscope. "And his breathing is a little ragged, but both are to be expected. He's strong." Jeremy stirred just then, moaning. Candy and Allyn tried to keep him still. Seconds later, Jeremy slowly opened his eyes and frowned as he tried to focus his vision.

"Candy," he whispered.

"Shhh, try to be quiet," she said.

"What...happened?" he persisted, squinting.

"Jeremy, just try to be quiet, please," Dr. Wright said firmly. Jeremy nodded and moaned. He closed his eyes but remained awake. Allyn quickly filled a hypodermic with morphine.

"This will ease the pain," she said as she injected the medication into Jeremy's arm.

"Thirsty," Jeremy murmured without opening his eyes. Allyn nodded and Candy poured some water into a cup, then handed it to the doctor. She gently raised Jeremy's head just enough for him to swallow a little bit of the water.

"That's enough for now," she said. "We'll see how you do with that." She eased Jeremy back down and he sighed shakily as a warmth spread throughout his body. After a few moments, he opened his eyes and even grinned at his wife.

"Better?" Allyn asked as Candy's face lit up in a smile. Jeremy stared at her for several moments before nodding his head to the doctor. It was then he noticed Jason, who came closer to the bed.

"Figures you'd find a way to get out of helping," he stated with a grin. Jeremy frowned and looked questioningly at his brother.

"Jason, may I see you outside...now?" Allyn asked.

"Of course. I'll be right back, Jeremy," Jason said. Jeremy nodded, sighed, and closed his eyes.

Jason followed Allyn outside the curtained room, puzzled by her sudden need to speak with him alone. When she spoke, it was in hushed tones so Jeremy would not hear.

"Jason, Jeremy probably doesn't remember much right now," she said. "He's suffered a lot of pain and that can dull memories. He's going to wonder about what you just said, so, please, when you go back in, just make something up. He doesn't need the strain of trying to remember all that's happened."

"All right, Allyn. *Will* he remember?"

"Eventually, once the pain has lessened. What did Sam tell you about Jeremy's chances?"

"He said a lot depended on how strong Jeremy is," Jason said somberly.

"Well, he is strong, Jason. But his wounds are deep and it's going to take some time and a lot of medication."

"I understand. Let's go back inside."

Jeremy was still awake when his brother and the doctor returned, but just barely. The morphine had made him floaty but hadn't quite put him to sleep yet. Jason placed a gentle hand on Jeremy's, grinning.

"Not sleepy, I see." Jeremy slowly shook his head and smiled in return. He wanted to talk but seemed to have very little control of his bodily functions. He frowned at Jason as if asking a question. "We've had a lot of work at camp," Jason went on. "Now, you get some rest, all right?" Jeremy nodded. "Good. I'll be back to see you later." Jeremy licked his dry lips as he closed his fingers around Jason's hand. His eyes closed and his hand relaxed. Dr. Wright quickly examined him and smiled.

"It's all right...he's asleep," she said softly. "May I suggest you both do the same?"

"I can't...not yet," Candy replied. "After I've had a chance to speak to the children, then maybe I will."

"They should be here soon, Candy. I'll wait, too," Jason said.

"All right," Allyn said. "I'm going to check on the other men. Get me if he wakes up again." Just as she finished speaking, they heard a loud commotion outside. Allyn and Jason went out to find out what was going on.

Some men were laying another man on one of the beds and Dr. Wright hurried over to them. After asking the others to leave, she immediately examined the injured man. She shouted for one of the nurses to assist.

The examination lasted only a few minutes, however. The doctor looked up at her assistant and sadly shook her head. She could do nothing for this patient.

"Sheila, please bring Chief Brandeis back in," she asked the nurse. Sheila went out and returned with the fire chief.

"You couldn't save him?" he asked.

"He probably died instantly, Evan," she explained.

"Yeah, that makes sense. There was an explosion and he was pretty close when it happened."

"Did he have any family?"

"None that we know of. Thanks for trying, Doc. Well, I guess we'd better set up a mortuary. I was hoping we wouldn't have need of that."

"Weren't we all? You'd better try and get him buried as soon as possible. In this heat, well…" Allyn covered the body.

"Yeah, I know what you mean." Brandeis went to the opening of the tent and motioned for a couple of men to come in. They came in, lifted the body, and left. Allyn looked up to see Jason coming toward her.

"First fatality, I'm afraid," she said.

"Let's hope there are no more," Jason said somberly.

"Yes, let's hope," Allyn replied, nodding toward where Jeremy lay.

Not long after, Kathryn and Jonathan arrived at the hospital tent, accompanied by Joshua and Callie. Kathryn hesitated before entering and turned to her uncle.

"Uncle Josh, would you mind if Jon and I go in first?" she asked.

"No, go ahead," he said quietly. As badly as he wanted to see his younger brother, Joshua felt the children had a greater need. "Callie and I'll wait out here. If Jason's still inside, please ask him to join us." Kathryn nodded, and she and Jonathan went inside.

Jason was just coming out of the curtained area when he spotted his niece and nephew. He smiled at them, albeit sadly. Jeremy still had a long road ahead to recovery.

"He's been awake once," he told them. "It's...going to take awhile."

"Uncle Josh would like to see you outside," Kathryn said, then hugged her uncle.

"Thanks. Your mother is with him, just down there." Jason pointed to the curtained off area. "I'll see you later." He left and Kathryn gave her brother an encouraging smile as they hurried to see their parents.

Jason emerged from the tent and joined Joshua and Callie. No one spoke for several moments. They looked down upon the smoldering remains of their city. Off in the distance, they saw the flames from the bank as it continued to burn.

"How's Jeremy?" Callie finally asked, smoothing out her skirt as she spoke. Joshua took her hand and gave it a small squeeze.

"He woke up once," Jason said. "He's in a lot of pain. Dr. Wright was able to help him, though. She says he won't remember much for a while. He's sleeping now."

"You think Douglas shot him, don't you?" Joshua asked as he gritted his teeth.

"Yeah."

"You're going to look for him...you two?" Callie asked, knowing the answer.

"Yes, Callie," Joshua replied. "We have to, even if it's just me and Jason."

"Count me in, Joshua," came the loud voice of Aaron Stempel. "I'll help as well."

"Thanks, Aaron," Jason said. "We could use it."

"Is Jeremy gonna be all right?"

"We don't really know yet. He was shot twice. The doctors say it'll be awhile before he's out of danger."

"I'm sorry, Jason, Josh. If there's anything else I can do—well, you know what I mean."

"Yes, we know. Thanks," Jason said.

"A prayer wouldn't hurt," Callie interjected.

"So, when do we get started?" Stempel asked.

"Well, we need to arm ourselves. We know for certain Douglas is armed," Joshua began.

"Josh, you don't know for certain that Douglas did shoot Jeremy," Callie protested. "How can you justify going after someone without knowing?"

"I think we ought to find him first, then ask questions," was her husband's tempered reply. "After all, he's the one who took off so suddenly at the church after making his crude accusations. So, he *does* have something to answer for."

"I suppose you're right there," Callie conceded. "But don't you want to wait until you know Jeremy is out of danger?" All three men fell silent as they contemplated her words. She seized the opportunity to talk some sense into them. "If you bide your time, Jeremy may be able to tell you who shot him. What if it was someone else?"

"She's right," Jason said, sighing. "I hate to go off on a chase to god knows where with Jeremy's life hanging in the balance. If…if he doesn't make it, I'd hate to…" He couldn't finish as tears welled up his eyes.

"He will make it, Jason," Joshua stated, a confidence in his voice. "But I agree to wait. I'd like to be here when he wakes up again."

"Well, I'll wait, too," Stempel said. "Why don't we go over and get some breakfast?"

"I think that's a good idea," Callie said. "Bring me something. I'm going to go in and see if Dr. Wright needs any help." Joshua hugged his wife then left with Jason and Stempel.

Candy sat quietly with her children. She had told them everything she knew about their father's condition. Jeremy was still asleep although he mumbled every now and then.

"My uncles are going to search for Jerome Douglas," Kathryn said.

"Yes, I knew they would," Candy said. "They aren't going this soon, are they?"

"I got the impression that they were."

"I can't believe they'd go off knowing Jeremy wasn't out of danger yet." Her voice took on an angry edge and she stood up. "I'll be right back. If your father wakes up, get Dr. Wright." Kathryn nodded, puzzled.

Candy went out of the area and saw Callie just coming inside the tent. Allyn stopped her before she could approach Joshua's wife, however. Candy assured the doctor that Jeremy was still asleep and that their children were with him. Then she went over to see Callie.

"Are Jason and Joshua still outside?" Candy asked.

"No," Callie replied and recognized the glint in Candy's eyes. "Don't worry, they're not going after Douglas just yet. I talked 'em into waiting."

"Oh good," Candy sighed. "I was ready to get all over them if they were. I mean, we don't know if Jeremy's going to—" She stopped and pressed her lips together.

"He's going to make it, Candy. We just have to have faith."

"Now you sound like Jason," she said and they both couldn't help but laugh a little.

"You look tired, Candy. Why don't you go home?"

"I think I will soon. Well, you see my in-laws, you just keep on making them wait. I'm going back inside." Callie nodded and Candy quickly went back to where her husband and children were.

"Mom," Jonathan said as soon as his mother was sitting beside him again, "Dad *is* gonna be okay, isn't he?"

"Oh, Jonathan, I hope so," she replied, hugging her small son.

"He will be, Jon," Kathryn stated. "Dad's a fighter...tough as they come!"

"You're right, he is!" Candy said. "Kathryn, what about Steven?"

"What about Mr. Fairfield?" she said coolly. "I haven't heard a word from him. Perhaps it's just as well."

"I don't believe that...and neither do you. He's just confused. You know, he reminds me of your father."

"Yeah, I know. Maybe when Dad's better—"

"Sooner," Candy interrupted. "I'm not in a hurry to get rid of you, but I think you need to go to him. That's something I learned long ago. It might not seem right, being the first one to bend, but it will."

"Maybe you're right, Mother. But right now, I think you ought to go home and get some rest. Now, no protests. You've been here a long time. Jon, take Mother home. I'll stay with Dad."

"I think I will go," Candy said with a sigh. "Come on, Jonathan. You're the man of the family for now."

"Does that mean I get to boss you around?" the ten-year-old asked excitedly.

"No, it does not," his mother replied with a soft laugh.

"Ah, nuts!" he shouted. Jeremy's mumblings grew louder but he didn't wake up.

"Let's go," Candy said quietly. "Your father needs to sleep, too." She leaned over Jeremy and softly brushed his forehead with her lips. "I love you," she whispered. Then she and Jonathan left Kathryn to watch over Jeremy.

Chapter Eleven

Candy quietly slipped her nightgown on then sighed as she looked in the full-length, oval mirror. Jeremy had sent off for it, all the way to St. Louis. It had been a present for Candy on their first wedding anniversary. As tears streamed down her face, she ran her fingers over the elegantly carved cherrywood. A lot of years had passed since she'd first met her husband.

She sat down on their bed and lay back. As she thought back to the first real conversation she'd had with Jeremy, she managed a smile. It had been on Clancey's old mule boat, close to the beginning of their long voyage to Seattle.

Candy hung out her laundry as some of the other brides, as the Bolt brothers called them, laughed and danced below her on the main deck of the *Shamus O'Flynn*. She shook her head and went back to her work. Her laundry basket tipped over as someone seemed to be climbing up to where she was. Candy quickly took the basket and leaned over to see Jeremy Bolt.

"Hello," she said cheerfully. Jeremy looked up at her, seemed to panic, and dropped down. Candy shrugged and went back to hanging her wash out. Jeremy climbed up again, all the way this time.

"Hey," he said as he pulled himself up. Candy said nothing but smiled. Jeremy stood up and brushed himself off, then leaned rather nonchalantly against a post. "I said hey," he repeated.

"That doesn't call for a comment, does it?" Candy asked.

"You been washin', huh?" he asked, sticking his hands in his pockets. Candy nodded.

"Could you hand me that corset?" she asked.

"C-C-uh, c-c-corset?"

"Corset, yes. Don't you know what a corset is?" She pulled one out of the basket and held it up. "Corset!" Jeremy turned away, embarrassed at first, then smiled and turned back. The ship suddenly rolled and Jeremy instinctively grabbed Candy to keep her from falling. She quickly stepped back and hung the corset on the line.

"Do, uh, do g-g-girls really-really wear that?" Jeremy asked shyly.

"'Course they do."

"Why?"

"So they won't wiggle." Candy giggled at that. Jeremy looked down at the people below.

"Uh, d-don't you c-care if, you know, people see you hang this out here?"

"They know I wear it; why shouldn't they know I wash it?"

"Yeah, that's right. To hell with 'em!" Jeremy's face colored with embarrassment. "Oh, excuse me, I'm sorry."

"No, you're right. To hell with them!" A silence settled on the couple momentarily. Jeremy took in a deep breath then spoke.

"I...st-st-stutter."

Candy didn't bat an eye as she replied, "I bite my nails." She held up her hand for Jeremy to see, and they both smiled at first, then snickered.

"Well, you-you better quit that. You bite too hard, you'll bleed to death!" Jeremy laughed.

"You stutter too much, you'll choke!" Candy retaliated. The ship suddenly rolled again, depositing Candy in Jeremy's arms. He hurriedly grabbed the laundry basket as if to help Candy. But they didn't work right away; they stood staring at each other for a very long time.

Jeremy nervously took Candy's hand in his as they walked past the dormitory. Her little brother and sister, Christopher and Molly, tried not to giggle as they watched the pair go off. Candy smiled as Jeremy played with her fingers.

"Are we walking to somewhere, or just walking?" she finally asked. It had been a long day for her and she was tired. She'd only recently received word that her mother had died.

"I guess we're walking till I get up enough nerve to say what I want to say," Jeremy replied with a nervous chuckle.

"Why don't you just say it?"

"All right," he whispered and led her to a nearby tree stump. "There's something you've gotta know, if you don't already. I love you and I want you to marry me." He chuckled again as Candy's eyes filled with tears. "That's not exactly how I meant to say it. I mean, I've been over it so many times in my mind and now when I get around to say it—"

"You said it beautifully," Candy quietly interrupted.

"Oh, Jeremy," Candy whispered. "You've just got to pull through this." She sat up on the bed and picked their wedding picture up off the nightstand. Holding it close to her heart, she lay back and sighed. As tired as she was, she finally drifted off into a restless slumber.

The next morning, Candy woke up feeling more refreshed than she thought she'd be. She hurriedly dressed and woke Jonathan up, then the two left to go see Jeremy. Jonathan complained that he was hungry and Candy said he could get something to eat at one of the tents.

After making sure her son was being taken care of, Candy quickly went over to the hospital tent. Allyn Wright was there, bright and early as usual. She stopped Candy to speak with her before she went in to see Jeremy.

"Get much sleep?" Allyn asked.

"Yes, more than I thought I would. Any change?"

"Some. He's been asleep all this time and that's a point in his favor. His fever's staying down, too. Send for me if he wakes up." Candy nodded and hurried on her way.

Kathryn smiled as her mother entered. Jeremy was quiet and a little color had come back into his face. He seemed absolutely tranquil, which told Candy that he was in a deep sleep.

"He's resting well. Dr. Wright was just here," Kathryn stated.

"Yes, I know. I just spoke with her." Candy sat beside her daughter and hugged her. "Did you get any sleep?"

"Oh yes. I came home, in fact, but you and Jon were sound asleep. I left early this morning."

"Good. Now, why don't you go see Steven? I understand he's in town at his business."

"I will. Jon still at home?"

"No, he's eating breakfast. I passed Richard on the way here, so I'm sure the two of them are together by now."

"Uh-oh, there may be nothing left to eat," Kathryn replied with a smile. She left soon after and Candy settled back, hoping that Jeremy would wake up soon.

Kathryn caught a ride with one of the workers going into the square. He was carrying food and other supplies for the others, who were diligently working at clearing away the burnt remains. Kathryn spotted Steven Fairfield, who was busy sifting through the ashes of what had once been his hardware store. Startled by her presence at first, he finally smiled.

"I'm sorry about your store," she said.

"Yeah, me too. How's your father?"

"You heard, huh?"

"I keep in touch. We sometimes worked together when the fire first broke out."

"Well, he's better, I think. He's still got a long way to go." She paused as she fought back her tears. "It's so hard."

"Yeah, I'm sure it is. Look, Katy, can we go somewhere and talk?"

"Of course. The park wasn't damaged. It should be pretty deserted at this hour."

"All right. I've got my wagon just over there," Steven pointed to where his wagon was.

"Let's go."

As they neared the park, Steven slowed the horse down and found a good spot to stop. Then he went around and helped Kathryn down. They walked to a quiet place and sat down.

"Katy," Steven began with a deep sigh, "I don't know where to begin. I'm sorry for acting like such an ass."

"Well, at least it would seem you don't believe I did anything 'improper,'" she replied, relieved.

"No, I don't. I guess I knew it all along, but when Douglas showed up, accusing you, I guess I allowed myself to doubt."

"It's normal to have doubts. I was just so angry with you. I really felt like you knew me better."

"I know. Forgive me?"

"I suppose," she said, then laughed. "I'm teasing. Of course I forgive you. I love you." Steven took her in his arms for a prolonged kiss. Kathryn sighed heavily and closed her eyes. Steven stroked her soft hair and smiled. It was good to be back together. "Was everything wiped out in the fire?" Kathryn asked.

"Practically. I managed to salvage some of my inventory. Guess I'm lucky I trade in tools and such. They'll need some cleaning up, but I think they'll do. It's just going to take some time."

"Well, I better get back to the hospital," she said, pulling away. "See how Dad is. Also, I want to see if my uncles have a plan for looking for Jerome Douglas."

"They think he's still around?"

"Yes. They think he shot Dad. And may have set the fire."

"Well, let's get you back then. Maybe I can help them search." The two stood up and walked back to the wagon, hand in hand.

They were both silent as Steven maneuvered the horse up the hill toward the hospital tent. Tension no longer existed between them, however, and they smiled and nodded to passersby along the way.

Steven waited outside as Kathryn went to see how her father was doing. She found no family member inside with him, but a nurse said he was still resting well. Her mother had been persuaded to go get something to eat. Kathryn went back outside to get Steven.

"Mother's gone over to eat. Would you like to go with me?" she asked him.

"Sure."

They quickly headed for the food tent and when Kathryn saw her uncles there as well, she smiled. Aaron Stempel also sat with them. Biddie produced a fresh pot of coffee and some sandwiches as the couple joined the family.

"How's Jeremy?" Steven asked.

"He's resting better," Candy replied, smiling at the young people in front of her. "He hasn't been awake again, though. Dr. Wright says that the sleep is good for him."

"Well, I'm sure she knows what she's talking about," Biddie said as she sat next to her best friend.

"I'll go sit with him, if you like," Steven volunteered.

"Thank you, Steven," Candy said. "But I feel better just being near him. I'm sure you two need some time together now."

"Oh my, yes," Biddie piped up. "Things are just getting better all the time!" She laughed, which made everyone at the table laugh.

"Katy, come with me?" Steven asked, holding out his hand to her.

"Of course." Kathryn gave her mother a hug. "I'll see you later, Mother." The couple started to leave when Allyn Wright came walking over.

"Well, this looks like a clan gathering," the doctor commented with a smile. "I'm glad you're together, though. Jeremy is awake and wants to see you." Candy needed no encouragement as she and the others followed Dr. Wright back to the hospital tent.

Once inside, she stopped the crowd with her. Jeremy was better but his condition still didn't allow for an overwhelming visitation. She spoke quietly to Candy.

"Candy, you go in first. One at a time, all right? I don't want him tired out."

"Of course, Allyn," Jason said. "Candy, we'll be right here."

"All right, Jason. I won't be long," Candy promised and went inside to see Jeremy. He smiled through half-shut eyes as she walked over to him. The nurse nodded to Candy then left.

"Feeling better?" she asked. Jeremy started to speak but she wouldn't let him. She placed a finger over his mouth and shook her head. "Just nod. Don't try to talk."

"It's all right, Candy," he said softly. "I...feel pretty tired, but I can talk."

"Oh Jeremy, I love you," she replied as tears quickly filled her eyes. She leaned over and gently kissed him.

"I love you, too," he said with a sigh. "I remember...some of what happened. Where's Jason?"

"He's waiting outside. I'll get him." Jeremy closed his eyes as Candy left.

Jason was quietly talking with Stempel when Candy emerged. She smiled and nodded for him to come in. He quickly followed her back inside. Candy sat down and Jason went to his brother's side. He gently patted Jeremy's hand before saying anything.

"I told...Candy I remember...some of what happened," Jeremy said quietly. Beads of perspiration formed on his face, so Jason knew he couldn't talk long.

"What do you remember?" he asked.

"Being at...the hotel and the fire." He paused and looked questioningly at Jason. "Seattle?"

"The fire's practically out now. Most of downtown is gone. Some of the other areas were hit, too. Do you remember being shot?"

"Yes," Jeremy replied with a nod. "It was...Douglas. He lied..." He closed his eyes as he paused and softly moaned. Jason hastily retrieved Dr. Wright. Then he and Candy watched as the doctor gave Jeremy another injection. She did a brief examination and sighed with relief as his wounds seemed to be healing well.

"You'll rest easier now, Jeremy," she said. "No more talking." He opened his misty eyes and slowly nodded. He sighed heavily as the medicine took effect. Allyn poured some water into a glass as he ran his tongue over his dry lips. She gently eased his head up so he could drink. He took only a couple of sips and lay back down. "Now, you go to sleep," Allyn instructed. "Someone will be with you if you need anything."

Jeremy closed his eyes and a few moments later, his breathing slowed down to an even rhythm.

"He's going back to sleep now," Allyn said softly. "I'll have a nurse stay with him. I want to talk to you outside."

Allyn waited until everyone sat down before she said anything else. Sighing heavily, she sat down as well.

"Jeremy is much better, I want to assure you of that. He's remembering events in bits and pieces and that's taking a toll on his strength. His memory of being shot is what concerns me most right now."

"Why?" Jason asked.

"It was such a violent act, Jason. And Jeremy suffered a lot of pain. He was helpless to stop Douglas. That's worrying him."

"Well, when he wakes up again, tell him we're going after Douglas."

"Is Jeremy...out of danger?" Candy asked.

"I think so. He's really quite strong and the wounds aren't bleeding any more than we would expect."

"Thank God," Candy breathed.

"Amen to that," Kathryn said.

"Yeah," Jason agreed. He stood up and the other men did likewise. "Well, I'm gonna go let Bennett know that Douglas *was* the person who shot Jeremy. Then we'll start looking for him."

"Good," Stempel said. "I'll go get a map of the territory. There's no telling where he might be."

"Steven and I will start asking around," Joshua offered. The women were soon alone again but their prayers went with the men.

Chapter Twelve

Jason, Joshua, and Stempel walked around by the city's waterfront, looking for clues. Jason spotted a man laying down on the ground, out cold. He tried to wake the man up while Joshua looked through a paper bag which was near the man.

"Jason, there are matches and a couple of small torches in here!" Joshua exclaimed.

"Somehow I can't believe that this bum could be responsible for the fire," Stempel said.

"Yeah," Jason said, unable to awaken the man. "This man smells like a distillery. Let's get him over to the jail. He could be responsible in part."

"You're still bettin' on Douglas?" Stempel asked.

"You got a better suspect?"

"No, no I don't."

They lifted the drunk and hauled him off to the jail. If nothing else, he'd at least sleep it off in a safer place.

Deputy Sheriff Ed Bennett locked the cell after the drunk was put inside on the cot. He shook his head and joined the men who'd brought the bum in. Bennett fingered the matches and torches.

"Thanks, Mr. Bolt—uh, Jason. He could be our firebug."

"Maybe, but I'm not sure," Jason replied.

"Well, we know he didn't shoot your brother. At least Jeremy was able to identify Douglas for that. But these homeless people are capable of a lot more than you would know."

"Ready, Jason?" Joshua asked impatiently. "We really should take advantage of the daylight while we can."

"Need any help?" Bennett asked.

"If you've got men to spare," Jason said. "I know you're spread pretty thin right now. We're going back over to the hotel, or what's left of it."

"We know that's where Jeremy...," Josh began, but his voice trailed as he couldn't find the words to finish. Jason patted his shoulder.

"That's where we're headed, Ed," Stempel said. "If you can send help, have them meet us there. Thanks."

"I'll do what I can," Bennett said. "Douglas almost killed Jeremy...that makes him a wanted man now." Jason nodded his thanks and left with Joshua, Stempel, and Steven.

Once outside, they mounted their horses and started off for the hotel ruins. They were met on the way by Christopher Pruitt, Candy's brother. He'd been away on family business but came back as soon as he'd heard about the fire.

"Well, well, disasters bring in all kinds," Joshua joked and took Christopher's extended hand.

"Thanks, I love you, too," Christopher said with a sneer. Then his voice betrayed concern with his next words. "I heard about Jeremy. How is he?"

"Better," Jason said. "Out of danger. We're just getting

ready to go searching for the man who shot him. You game?"

"You bet." He turned his horse around and followed the others.

By sunset, the men felt they were close. A man fitting Douglas' description had been seen around the Chinese district over the last couple of days. It seemed pretty stupid that he would still be hanging around Seattle.

"I would have thought he'd at least head for Canada," Bennett said. He'd joined the search party a few hours earlier.

"That thought crossed our minds, but it doesn't look that way," Stempel stated. "He was last seen heading through here. I don't think he's that far ahead of us."

"He's not in any hurry," Christopher said. "Maybe he thinks Jeremy's dead."

"Makes sense," Joshua said thoughtfully. "If Jeremy had died, no one could positively identify Douglas as the killer." He looked around then spoke again. "Jason, maybe we should split up and spread out. There are a lot of places he could be if he's holed up in this area."

"You're right, Josh. All right. You, Steven, and Christopher come with me. Aaron, you go with the deputy."

"Right," Stempel said. "Watch yourselves. We know he's armed." The men split up and fanned out. If Douglas was hiding out in the Chinese district, he'd have to show sooner or later.

In an apartment above a Chinese grocery, Jerome Douglas quickly packed his belongings. He'd heard that Jeremy Bolt had survived and there was now a search party out looking for him. He looked up as a small man entered through the open door.

"Better to leave now," he said quietly.

"Yeah, yeah," Douglas muttered. "I'm ready." He tossed some bills on the bed. "There, I'm paid up." The Oriental man bowed politely but Douglas just brushed past him on the way out.

Douglas cautiously looked about as he walked away from the laundry. He continuously watched around him; the livery was only a few blocks away.

Inside the livery, however, a trap was being set. Jason, Joshua, Christopher, and Steven waited behind one of the stalls while Stempel and Bennett kept watch outside the building.

"Good thing Mr. Wong knew who we were looking for," Joshua said quietly.

"Yeah," Steven murmured.

"Good thing Mrs. Wong keeps house for me," Jason said wryly. "Quiet now."

Outside, Stempel and Bennett were hidden by the building but able to see Douglas as he slowly approached. Bennett nodded and Stempel headed around the back to let the others inside know.

He entered the livery through a back door and joined the others. He nodded and they all took their places. They had to leave Douglas a wide berth.

The front door opened and Douglas slowly entered. His eyes narrowed as he looked around. Keeping his gun in front of him, he walked over to his horse. After setting his satchel down on the ground, he started to inspect the other stalls, when Bennett flung the front doors open, shouting,

"Put the gun down, Douglas! Don't even think of trying anything...you can't win!" Douglas turned at the sound of the other men coming out of the stalls. It took only a second to decide it would be futile to shoot. He threw his gun down and held his arms above his head. Bennett quickly cuffed him.

Kathryn had persuaded her mother to take a break and get some dinner. Jeremy was sound asleep again after having been awake for a short time earlier in the day. He seemed to be improving at a rate the doctors found satisfactory.

Kathryn saw her uncles first and poked Candy in the arm to get her attention. Candy looked around and felt relieved at the sight of her family. The smiles on their tired faces told her they had good news.

"Well, it's over. Douglas is in jail," Jason said and sat down.

"No one hurt?" Candy asked, pouring him a cup of coffee.

"Nope. How's Jeremy?" Joshua asked.

"He's resting better. He was awake for a little while this afternoon. Dr. Michaels is in with him now, but he was asleep when Kathryn and I left."

"Hey, Sis," Christopher said, giving Candy a big hug.

"When did you get back? How's Molly?" she asked.

"Late this morning. And Molly's fine. She sends her love. Says she'll come out as soon as she can. I ran into this search party and joined 'em. I'm glad Jeremy's gonna be okay."

"So are we," Kathryn said and smiled as Steven sat next to her.

"Well, I'm going home," Christopher said. "I'll tell you how the trip went later." Candy nodded and watched as her brother scooped up a couple of sandwiches and left.

"Did Callie go home?" Joshua asked.

"Yes, Uncle Josh. She said she'd be back, though."

"Well, I'm going to go home, too. I'll be back later." Joshua kissed Candy's forehead and headed outside.

"Katy?" Steven asked as he stood up.

"Coming. I'll relieve you in a while, Mother," Kathryn said. She and Steven left as well.

"Well, that looks promising," Stempel stated as he poured himself another cup of coffee.

"Yes, it does," Candy agreed. "I think we'll have a wedding soon." She stood up and turned to Jason. "What about Douglas?"

"He hasn't talked, Candy. Bennett can hold him indefinitely, though. As soon as Jeremy is able, he'll have to sign the complaint of attempted murder. But Douglas won't admit to anything."

"Don't worry, Candy," Stempel said. "He can't hurt anyone now."

"Want me to come with you?" Jason asked.

"No, you should go home and get some rest, both of you.

Besides, you know how selfish I am when it comes to Jeremy." Candy smiled and the two men nodded and exchanged knowing smiles.

Callie emerged from the kitchen just as Joshua entered the house. He was sweaty and dirty but she didn't care. He was alive and okay.

"Are you all right? How's Jeremy?" she asked.

"Whoa! One thing at a time," he replied and smiled as he looked into Callie's strikingly clear blue eyes. "I'm fine and Jeremy is better. We caught Douglas and he's in jail."

"Hungry?"

"Yeah, a little. I'm gonna get cleaned up while you fix something. Then I want to go back and visit with Jeremy."

"Of course. I have water already heated if you want to take a bath."

"That sounds good. Where are your glasses?"

"I need you to tighten them up for me. They're too loose again."

"Maybe we should look at getting a new pair."

"Maybe. Come on, I'll pour the water for you." He followed her into the kitchen to retrieve the hot water.

Joshua and his family got back to the hospital tent a couple of hours later. They found the rest of the Bolt clan together, waiting.

"Any word?" Joshua asked.

"Not yet. Dr. Michaels is examining Jeremy now. He's awake though," Jason said.

"And Dr. Wright did say he's out of danger," Candy added.

"That's wonderful, Candy," Callie said. They all turned as Dr. Michaels walked toward them. He smiled and nodded his head, then they followed him back.

Jeremy smiled as his family entered, but he remained quiet. He was tired, especially after the examination. But he was feeling better, without the aid of morphine, so far.

"Daddy, Steven and I have an understanding again," Kathryn said.

"Doesn't that have a familiar ring?" Candy asked and Jeremy grinned and nodded. Steven looked at Jason, who nodded.

"Jeremy, we caught Douglas. He's in jail," he said.

"Good," Jeremy said, sighing.

"Bennett has telegraphed the marshal in Olympia. Douglas will be taken there for trial. You don't have to attend, Jeremy. Bennett has a paper for you to sign, that's all," Jason revealed.

"I'm sorry, Jeremy, Candy, for ever doubting Katy," Steven said. "I should've known—"

"It's all right," Jeremy interrupted. "You don't have to apologize to us."

"I've already apologized to Katy," the young man replied, taking Kathryn's hand.

"So, when's the wedding?" Joshua asked.

"When Daddy's well enough to give me away...again!"

"Think you can wait...that long?" Jeremy asked, grinning.

"I think so," his daughter replied. "It won't be all that long anyway. You'll be up and out of here soon."

"That's right!" Jonathan added. Jeremy smiled at his children.

"What about...Seattle, Jason? I mean, cleanup..."

"Well, the cleanup has already begun. There's going to be a town meeting in a few days. Chief Brandeis wants to be sure the danger is past. It's been so dry lately that I think he's afraid some of the embers could spark again. So, he's got his men sifting through the ashes to make sure they put out anything that's glowing."

"Maybe I can go to the meeting," Jeremy said.

"I don't know about that, Jeremy," Michaels stated. "You're going to stay in the hospital for quite a while. No protests."

"Don't worry, Doctor," Candy said. "He'll stay put."

"She's in charge." Jeremy sighed but grinned.

"There'll be plenty left to do by the time you're out of here, Jeremy," Jason said.

"How's Clancey?" Candy asked.

"Clancey?" Jeremy said, puzzled. "What—"

"He's fine…in body," Jason said quietly. "The ship's gone."

"He's just so quiet, Jason," Joshua said. "He didn't even turn down your offer to stay with you."

"Do you…do you think he'll be all right?" Jeremy asked, his chin quivering just a bit. He knew how much the ship had meant to the old sea captain.

"I don't know, Jeremy," Jason replied honestly. "I think so. Josh is right though. Clancey has been very quiet…and sober. Even when Lottie died, he at least talked to us afterwards."

"He just needs time," Candy said softly. "I'm sure he'll be all right."

"All right, that's all the time you get, Jeremy," Michaels said. "Ann is bringing you some broth and I want you to try to keep some down, all right?"

"All right, I'll try. I don't feel hungry, though."

"I know, but do try." The doctor turned to the others then. "I want all of you to go home and get some rest, too. You can come back in the morning."

"I'll see…you tomorrow," Jeremy said, grinning. Kathryn and Jonathan gave him a kiss; Jason, Joshua, and Callie patted his arm. Candy lingered as the others left. Then she leaned over her husband and gave him a brief kiss.

"I'll see you in the morning," she said. "I love you."

"I love you…too."

"This should hit the spot," Ann announced, carrying a tray in.

"I'm not…sure about that," Jeremy said, wrinkling his nose.

"Well, you do as she says," Candy ordered. Jeremy nodded, grinning again. Candy left as the nurse got Jeremy positioned to drink the soup.

Chapter Thirteen

Two days later, Candy walked into the hospital tent to find Jeremy no longer inside the curtained area. He had been moved closer to the front of the tent that morning; he was even sitting up.

"Well, look at you!" Candy exclaimed.

"Progress, huh?" Jeremy said, beaming. "Good morning." Candy carefully hugged him then pulled up a chair.

"How are you feeling?"

"Much better. Dr. Wright says she's going to move me to the regular hospital tomorrow. I like it here, though...fresh air."

"I'm sure she knows best. Hungry?"

"No. I've already had breakfast...what they'll let me have." He shuddered and added, "I'm not sure what it was!"

"Well, at the rate you're improving, you'll be eating real

food soon." Candy laughed.

"I think you're right, Candy," Allyn Wright stated. "How are you feeling?"

"Rested," Candy replied, nodding. "A real night's sleep makes a difference."

"Good," Jeremy said softly, frowning. "I'm sorry I've caused you so much worry, Candy."

"Jeremy!" she said, surprised. "You stop talking nonsense. You couldn't have known—"

"Yes, I could have," he stated. "I knew Douglas was out there, waiting. I saw him earlier that night." Candy said nothing as this bit of news was revealed. Jeremy went on. "And I knew he was armed. I could've gone back with Josh instead of staying at the hotel alone. Josh and I got into it about that very thing. You know how stupid I get when I'm angry."

"Yes, I know," Candy said, shaking her head. "Your temper hasn't gotten worse over the years, but no better either." She laughed at that and Jeremy sneered at her.

"Thanks for the support, wife!" he said. "Anyway, there was a lot I could have done to prevent what happened."

"Maybe. Even if you had done things differently, he could have still shot you…he could have killed you," Candy said quietly. That fact sent a cold chill through her and she placed her hand on Jeremy's. "Those first couple of days were hard," she added as tears misted over her eyes.

"I'm sure they were," Jeremy whispered, frowning again. He grunted a little as he tried to get more comfortable. Sitting up was proving to be very tiring. He sighed heavily then looked back at his wife. "I *am* sorry, Candy. I suppose there's not much point belaboring the issue."

"No," she replied, brightening a bit. "And Douglas will be going to Olympia soon."

"At least he can't hurt Kathryn anymore." He grinned then and held Candy's hand. "I'm glad she and Steven got things worked out."

"They're just waiting for you to recover. They've been together a lot these last couple of days." Just then, Kathryn and

Jonathan entered the tent and were notably surprised at what they saw.

"Oh, Daddy, you look wonderful!" Kathryn exclaimed.

"Well, I don't know about that," Jeremy replied, scratching the stubble on his face. "But I feel much better."

"I'll be glad when you're home," Jonathan said.

"So will I, pal. It won't be much longer."

"If you'll excuse me for just a few minutes, I need to examine my patient," Allyn said. "It won't take long." The family left and the doctor did a brief check on Jeremy's wounds. She smiled as she removed the bandages. "Well, they look good. You've been behaving."

"I haven't had any other choice," Jeremy said, chuckling.

"True enough. I understand you ate all of your delicious breakfast."

"I wouldn't call it that," he said, making a terrible face, "but yes, I did."

"Any pain?"

"Some...not too bad. Takes a lot longer to heal these days, I guess."

"Well, we're not as young as we used to be. You were *very* lucky, Mr. Bolt."

"I know. Thanks to Dr. Michaels and you, I'm still here."

"Well, you have taken pretty good care of yourself over the years, Jeremy, and that accounts for your fast recovery as well. We doctors can only do so much with our knowledge and the medicines available to us."

"Now, I'm going to put on clean bandages and give you a shot."

"Could I have the medicine first?" Jeremy asked.

"Of course. Pain a little stronger than you thought?"

"Something like that. Thanks." Jeremy watched as Allyn prepared the hypodermic and noticed that she didn't fill the syringe this time. He sighed with relief as the numbing liquid was injected. A familiar warmth quickly spread through his body and he closed his eyes for a moment. Allyn changed the bandages then arranged the pillows so Jeremy could lie back.

He'd sat up long enough.

"Better?" she asked and he nodded without opening his eyes. Even knowing he hadn't been given as much pain medication, it definitely took the edge off. He opened his eyes finally and grinned.

"Thanks. Can I ask you a question?"

"Of course."

"How come you didn't give me as much this time?"

"I didn't think you needed as much," she replied, surprised. "Do you?"

"No, I'm fine. I just wondered."

"Well, if you do need more, let me or someone else know. There's no point in you being in pain. All right?"

"All right. I feel pretty good now."

"Good. How's the shoulder?"

"Fine. Having it in this sling helps a lot."

"I want you to move it for me," she said as she gently slipped his right arm out of the cloth sling. Jeremy gritted his teeth as he slowly lifted his arm up. He was able to raise it a few inches. "Good. Now, slowly lower it back down, but don't let it just drop," Allyn instructed. Jeremy did so with little strain. Allyn placed his arm back in the sling and smiled. "Any tingling or numbness?" she asked.

"My fingers tingle a little," he admitted as he wiggled them.

"Give them a minute to rest, then see if they do." Jeremy nodded and the doctor went outside the tent for a minute.

"Candy, I'd like to talk to you," Allyn said as she sat next to Jeremy's wife and children.

"Is he all right?" Candy quickly asked.

"He's fine. We're going to start giving him real food tonight, but I'm a little worried about his color. He lost a lot of blood and Dr. Michaels and I wanted to wait awhile…see if Jeremy would be all right without a transfusion."

"Does he need one?"

"I still want to wait and see. We'll monitor him and run a blood test in the next day or two. If his blood cell count is still down by then, I may need to transfuse."

"All right. I know his brothers have both offered," Candy said, smiling a little.

"I know what cells are," Jonathan stated proudly. "We learned about them in school."

"Very good, Jonathan," Dr. Wright said, smiling. "Well, I needed to let you know about this. I didn't want you to be in the dark.

"Jeremy is a fast healer, but he still needs to be reminded that he's not a young man anymore. The older the body gets, the longer it takes to repair itself."

"Don't worry, we'll remind him," Kathryn said with a laugh. "I've always wanted to tell him he's an old man!"

"Well, we won't tell him that," Candy said sternly. "He isn't an old man yet. But I understand what you're saying, Doctor. Once he's feeling better, he's likely to overdo it."

"I'm sure you'll keep him in line."

"I'll... we'll do our best. Does he know about the possibility of a blood transfusion?"

"No, not yet. I wanted to speak with you first. I'll go in and talk to him about it, then you can come back in. I had to give him something for pain, but he should be able to stay awake for a little while yet." She got up and went back inside then.

Jeremy opened his eyes when he heard the rustle of the doctor's skirts. He even grinned at his ability to detect her presence. The morphine definitely erased the pain and that allowed him to focus on other things.

"Hi," he said, grinning.

"Feeling pretty good, huh? How're the fingers now?"

"All right, no tingling."

"Good." Allyn sat down beside her patient before going on. "I've had a long talk with Candy about your condition."

"Oh?"

"You're doing well, don't worry," she assured him. "But I would like to see more color to your skin. You'd lost a lot of blood by the time you were brought in. Dr. Michaels and I both felt it best to wait awhile before making any kind of decision on a transfusion."

"You mean you wanted to see if I was really going to make it, don't you?" Jeremy asked, his blue eyes narrowing.

"I suppose that was part of it. But someone in your good physical condition can sometimes recover quite rapidly, even under severe circumstances. And you're certainly not an old man, by any means."

"And now? Do I need a transfusion?"

"I don't know yet. I'll know by tomorrow. What we've been feeding you, while not very tasty, is loaded with iron, which is essential for restoring the blood. Tonight, you're going to have a little bit of beef. It'll pretty much be like a paste, but do try and keep it down."

"I'll do my best. Thank you for being honest with me."

"It's only fair to keep you informed."

"Well, you've always been fair, Dr. Wright." Jeremy took her hand in his and gave it a gentle squeeze.

"Pretty firm grip you've got there, Mr. Bolt," she said, smiling. "We'll see what the tests show tomorrow, all right?"

"All right," Jeremy murmured. He blinked several times, trying to stay awake. "Could...could I see my family now? I'm really...sleepy."

"Of course. I'm sure Candy will be here even if you're asleep."

"I'm sure."

Allyn quickly went to get the family and ushered them inside, then left to check on her other patients.

"Pretty sleepy, Dad?" Jonathan asked.

"Yeah."

"You go on to sleep, then," Candy said, sitting beside her husband. "We can always talk. You need your rest. I'll be right here."

"I...told Dr. Wright...you would..." Jeremy sighed heavily and gave in to the medication completely. Candy stroked his damp hair back and smiled. Of the one hundred women who'd made the voyage west so long ago, Candy thought she had been the luckiest. She had found Jeremy.

Chapter Fourteen

Aaron Stempel sat almost rigidly across from Jason Bolt that afternoon. He'd come at Jason's request, knowing full well what the meeting was going to be about. Stempel hadn't been wrong and now the two men were doing what they did best—argue.

"Oh, come on, Aaron!" Jason yelled. "You know I'm right!"

"Bolt, I can understand your point but—"

"But what? You need to clear up this problem about the water line as soon as possible!"

"I suppose I do," Stempel said with a sigh. "Jason, you know I wouldn't have deliberately cut corners on something this important to Seattle's growth just to save a few dollars."

"Nah, no, of course not. And anyone who knows you,

knows you wouldn't have. The problem is, you've got to explain it and show your documentation on the project to prove it."

"All right. I'll get the receipts and the project blueprints to the mayor right away. That should clear up any misconceptions."

"I'll go with you, if you like."

"Thanks, Bolt. I'd appreciate your support. I still can't believe the pipes weren't laid all the way through."

"Yeah. Somebody will have to answer for it. At least it won't be you."

"At least. In part anyway...I *was* the project leader. I'll bear some of the responsibility. Well, I'd better get those papers together. How about going with me tomorrow?"

"Fine. Josh went to Auburn today but should be back sometime tonight, tomorrow morning at the latest. I want to see Jeremy first light, though."

"All right. Say, how is Jeremy?"

"He'd lead you to believe he's ready to go home." They both nodded and laughed at that.

Later that evening, Jason changed his mind about waiting until morning to pay his little brother a visit. As he walked into the tent, he found he was just in time to see Jeremy being readied for a move.

"Well, is your best patient leaving you?" he asked Dr. Michaels.

"No, just being transferred to the main hospital."

"I don't see why I can't just stay here," Jeremy said, a sullen look on his face.

"Because we're dismantling the tent, Jeremy," Michaels said with a disgusted sigh. "How many times must we go through this? We don't need to be here anymore. The fire is completely out. You're the only patient that still needs hospitalization."

"Need any help?" Jason asked, smirking.

"Yeah, keep him quiet."

"Ah, Doc!" Jeremy exclaimed.

"Now, Jeremy," Jason said quietly, "you'll be more comfortable in a regular hospital bed. Besides, I bet they'll give you a room with a view of the mountain."

"That wouldn't be too bad," Jeremy decided. "Doc?"

"I'll see what we can do." The doctor shook his head and nodded to two orderlies. "All right, let's move him."

"See ya up there, Jason," Jeremy said. Jason nodded as Jeremy was carefully lifted onto a litter. He'd been given a mild sedative to make the journey more comfortable. Michaels told Jason that his brother would probably be asleep by the time they got him settled in. Jason mounted his horse and followed behind the hospital wagon.

Jason awoke to a loud knocking on his door late that night. He sleepily pulled on his pants and went to see who it was. He yawned as he let Joshua inside.

"Sorry, Jason. I never knew you to retire so early."

"Well, it's been a long day, Josh. So, have we got the extension on the McDaniel contract?"

"Got anything to drink?"

"Joshua..." Jason eyed his brother warily.

"Oh, we got the extension." Joshua headed for Jason's kitchen with his brother close behind. After rummaging through the cupboards, Joshua turned around. "Haven't you got a bottle?"

"No, I think Clancey found them all. Now, Joshua, what's going on? I've never known you to be in such a hurry for a drink."

"Well, I found out about a new contract being offered by the owner of Noonan Shipping while I was in Auburn. And I understand that Aaron Stempel is interested in the deal as well."

"Aaron mentioned something about it. But I'm not sure we could handle another contract right now. We got behind on the McDaniel project because of the fire. And there's a lot that needs to be done just recovering from the fire."

"I guess you're right," Joshua said, sitting down. "I guess

I got a little carried away."

"Why? What did you do?" Jason sat down as well.

"Well, I, uh, I put the Bolt Brothers in as a possible bidder." Jason opened his mouth to speak but Josh was quicker. "That doesn't mean we're obligated or anything like that. It just means that Noonan will come out to see our operation, if he's interested."

"And, if he is, just when would that visit take place?"

"Next month, sometime around the first."

"Joshua," Jason sighed and stood up. "I can't believe you'd do something like this. Not with everything that's happened."

"I got excited and…a few drinks helped," Joshua admitted with a shrug. "Look, Jason, I know there's a lot to do. But listen," he paused as an idea came to him, "if Noonan does want us to fill his order, we could put Jeremy in charge. He'll probably be well enough to handle the desk by then, don't you think? I mean, I know he won't be able to do physical labor anymore—"

"Now hold on, Josh," Jason interrupted. "Jeremy's not going to be reduced to being behind the desk. He's going to make a full recovery."

"Jason, we've got to face facts here. Jeremy was hurt…bad. Remember what Michaels said about his arm? He'd have limited use of it. And the bullet that went into the middle of his chest…"

"It missed his heart."

"Barely. Jason, if Jeremy overdid it, just once, we'd lose him. I don't want that to happen. Do you?"

"No, of course not. Allyn said it would take a long time for Jeremy to completely recover, but that he would. We can't just go to him and say, 'Sorry, Brother, but you're gonna have to sit this one out.' And then the next, and the next—"

"Jason, that's not what I'm saying. We'll help him, although that could be tough. He does have the Bolt temper." Jason couldn't help but laugh at that, nodding. "Jeremy's about as tough as God makes 'em. I know that, in time, he'll be physically fit again. But until that time—"

"Let's talk this over with him before we decide anything, all right?"

"All right. Jason, it's one of the biggest contracts offered in a long time. I think we ought to at least consider it. And if Stempel is willing to put up some of the cost, then—"

"We'll consider it, Josh. Now, you should get home to your family and I should get back to bed.

"Jeremy was moved to the regular hospital today."

"Ahead of schedule, huh? I bet he's happy about that."

"Not really. I think he wants to go home."

"Yeah. Has Douglas been moved to Olympia yet?"

"Not yet. Bennett's waiting for the marshal's deputies to arrive. They should be here in a day or two."

"Oh. Well, I'll see you in the morning. 'Night, Jason."

"Good night, Josh. I want us—you and me—to go see Jeremy first thing, all right?"

"Sure. See you at the hospital then." Jason nodded and Joshua left. Jason stopped by the guest room to check on Clancey, who was still sound asleep. Jason shook his head; Clancey was still not talking much to anyone.

Deputy Sheriff Bennett walked inside his office before dawn the next morning. He sent his night deputy on home, after he'd fixed a fresh pot of coffee. Bennett never had made a good pot.

He sat down and got a couple of swallows down when Jerome Douglas began a loud racket. Bennett just shook his head and disregarded the noise. Douglas yelled louder until the deputy had to do something about it. He unlocked the outer door that led to the cells.

"All right, all right!" he shouted impatiently. "What's the prob—" Two men quickly grabbed him and disarmed the deputy. One man took the keys and opened Douglas' cell. As Douglas hurried out to collect his guns and other belongings, the other two men tied Bennett up and gagged and shoved him into a cell. Bennett could hear their laughter as they left.

Biddie climbed out of the buggy while Essie Gustafson kept the horse still. Reaching back in for a large basket, Biddie nodded to the retired schoolteacher and smiled.

"Thanks for the ride in, Essie," she said.

"No problem. Are you sure you won't need a ride home?"

"No. Melissa will be by later. I still can't believe she's old enough to have a gentleman caller."

"It has been a long time. But don't you worry...Olaf will see to it that Peter acts properly."

"Oh, I'm sure of that," Biddie said with a nervous laugh. She'd known Essie and Olaf for many years and she knew their son was a gentleman, but it was Biddie's nature to worry.

"Well, then, if you're all right here, I'll take the other supplies up to the relief tents. Say hello to the sheriff for me."

"I'll do that." Biddie turned and went up the steps to the sheriff's office. It was very quiet as she entered. She set the basket down and started to leave when she heard a noise coming from where the cells were. "Hello," she called out. She heard the noise again and timidly went over to the outer door. It was open and she cautiously stuck her head around it. Her eyes widened and she ran to where the deputy was.

Jason and Joshua casually strode into the hospital but had to wait to see their brother. His doctor was examining him and they could not be interrupted. A desk clerk offered the two Bolt brothers coffee, which they graciously accepted.

Inside his room, Allyn Wright had just finished checking Jeremy's wounds. Jeremy could tell by the look on her face that she was pleased with what she saw. But he waited for her to talk.

"Well, you're improving quite rapidly. Any pain?" she asked.

"A little...not much. So, about the blood tests?"

"Good news," she said, smiling. Jeremy blew out a breath of relief. "But you're going to be with us for some time yet, understood?"

"Yes ma'am," he replied, trying not to smirk.

"I was glad to see that you were able to keep your dinner down. Chest wounds can make it difficult sometimes. But, as I've said before, you were very lucky."

"What about my arm?"

"I think we'll start with some physical exercise today. It may be a little painful at first, but as your muscles strengthen, you'll do better."

"Thanks. I think I can handle a little pain now. To tell you the truth, I'd started looking forward to the shots. And I don't want that."

"Wise man, Mr. Bolt. Morphine can be habit forming. But if you feel the need for something, you let us know. Constant pain can hamper recovery."

"All right. When's breakfast?"

"Soon," Allyn said, smiling. "And I believe you have a couple of visitors as well. Feel up to seeing them?"

"Of course. Thanks again, Dr. Wright."

"It must be imbedded in your nature!" she exclaimed.

"What?" Jeremy looked at her questioningly.

"You and your brothers are always thanking me!"

"Oh, well, we-we're grateful," Jeremy replied, blushing. Allyn patted his left arm and smiled.

"I do like it," she said and Jeremy grinned, nodding. "Well, I'll send your visitors in and I'll see you later."

"Well, well, I'd say the move agreed with you," came Jason's booming baritone. Jeremy grinned.

"Mornin'," he acknowledged.

"I think he's even got a little color, don't you, Jason?" Joshua asked with a laugh.

"Josh, how was Auburn?" Jeremy asked as his brothers pulled chairs alongside the bed.

"Good. We got the extension. And I found out about another contract available."

"Oh?" Jeremy looked at Jason curiously. "I didn't think we could handle anything new yet."

"We can't...not right away," Joshua confirmed. "I just put

our names in the hat as a possibility. If they're interested, they'll send someone out for a look-see first of July." Jeremy nodded and Joshua went on. "We—I figured you'd probably be well enough by then to be spokesman."

"I would think so. I know I won't be much help otherwise."

"You will be...it just takes time," Jason said.

"I don't know, Jason. I'm not sure I'll ever do anything physically hard again." Jeremy looked down at that and sighed.

"I wouldn't complain." Joshua tried to make light of the situation. "I'm gettin' too old for hard work!" Jeremy looked up at his brother like he was crazy, then slowly, his lips curled upward and he shook his head.

"I see your point, Josh," he said at last and Jason grinned, relieved to see Jeremy's sense of humor return so quickly.

"Jeremy, what do the doctors have to say?" he asked.

"Well, I don't need a transfusion."

"Thank God," Joshua breathed.

"Amen," Jeremy replied. "I'm supposed to start some exercises later today, for my arm. Now, how are you guys holding up?"

"Pretty well, considering all that's happened," Jason said, patting Jeremy's hand.

"I understand Kathryn and Steven got things worked out," Joshua said, smiling.

"Yeah. They—" Jeremy was interrupted by Allyn Wright as she came rushing into his room. She paused a moment to catch her breath but the men knew by the look on her face that she was genuinely frightened.

"Allyn, what is it? What's wrong?" Jason asked. He took her by the arm but she would have no part of his gallantry.

"I just heard that Douglas escaped," she stated. "Biddie found Bennett tied and gagged, and locked in a jail cell. Two men busted Douglas out. Bennett is out looking for them now but…"

"But, you think he'll come here?" Jeremy asked as he sat

up straight. "I don't think he'll come after me, not yet." Then a look of fear crossed his face and he turned to his brothers. "Kathryn!" he shouted, wincing as he did so.

"Don't worry, Jeremy, I'll go get her. And Candy and Jonathan, too," Jason stated. "I think Kathryn's with Steven. Josh?"

"I'll stay with Jeremy, just in case," Josh replied as he helped Jeremy lay back. "Douglas has to know by now that Jeremy didn't die."

"All right. Joshua, I've got a gun in my office. I'll get it," Allyn Wright said and turned to leave.

"Allyn, I'm surprised," Jason said.

"It's just a little derringer, but it holds two bullets. It's something," she replied with a shrug and hurried off.

"Jason, please hurry!" Jeremy said loudly, anxious. Jason nodded and practically ran out of the room.

Chapter Fifteen

Bennett and three of his deputies managed to catch the two men who had helped Douglas escape. They refused to tell where Douglas had gone, however. The deputies hauled the prisoners off to jail while Bennett headed for Jeremy Bolt's house. He, like Jeremy, figured Kathryn Bolt would be Douglas' target and not Jeremy. Bennett also knew that even if he were wrong and Douglas did go after Jeremy, the other two Bolt brothers would safeguard their brother.

As he spurred his horse on, Bennett ran into Steven Fairfield and Christopher Pruitt, who quickly told the deputy about having spotted someone fitting Douglas' description in town, near the bank. The walls of the building had withstood the onslaught of the blaze days earlier, and so had the main safe.

"Steven, I think you need to go to your fiancée's house," Bennett began.

"Jason has already taken Jeremy's family to the hospital," said Steven.

"All right then, let's go see if Douglas is playing it stupid," Bennett said. "I can't believe he would be, but it won't hurt to check it out."

The three men dismounted as soon as they saw the fire chief headed toward them. He was shaking his head and Bennett stood beside his horse, ready to ride again.

"Chief?" he asked.

"A man fitting Douglas' description went around the remains of the courthouse," Brandeis stated. "We caught the man, but it isn't Douglas. Sorry."

"All right, thanks. Can you take him to the jail for me? I'm going to head up to the hospital," Bennett said. Brandeis nodded and walked away. Bennett turned to Steven and Christopher. "Would you men be willing to be deputized?" Both men nodded. "Good. Consider yourselves such!"

"I'll get a couple of other men and go over to Jeremy's house," Christopher volunteered. "Douglas shouldn't know for sure where Jeremy is. But he might figure Kathryn's at home."

"All right. Good thinkin', Chris. Steven, you coming with me?"

"You bet." Christopher quickly mounted and took off while the deputy and Steven turned their horses southward.

Christopher and four of his friends from the logging camp cautiously made their way up the hill to his sister's house. One of the men had spotted a rider going that way, just ahead of them. Only two of the men had rifles, but hopefully that would be enough.

Jerome Douglas rode around to the back of the house, jumped off the stolen horse, and kicked the back door in. To his surprise, there seemed to be no one home. Gun drawn, he was still cautious as he searched every room. After coming up empty, he was angrier than ever. He would have Kathryn Bolt. And he'd make sure anyone he left for dead this time was as dead as Abe Lincoln.

"There's his horse," one of the men whispered as he and the others dismounted behind the coachhouse.

"Easy now, we know he's armed," Christopher said. "We'll just wait him out. Soon as he finds no one home, he won't waste any time gettin' outta here."

Candy and Kathryn had to hurry to keep up with Jason's long stride as they headed for Jeremy's room. They met with curious stares as they reached their destination.

"Thank God you're all right," Jeremy said, heaving a sigh of relief at the sight of them. "Where's Jon?" he asked, not seeing his son.

"He's all right, Jeremy, calm down," Candy said, sitting beside him. "He's with Richard and Callie."

"I'm sure Douglas won't think to go to my house," Joshua said confidently.

"No, I wouldn't think he would," Jeremy said as he lay back. "But I don't think he's stupid either." He looked at his daughter and asked, "Didn't you say he worked with federal lawmen?"

"Yes. I'm sure Jon is all right, Dad," she replied, sitting on the other side of the bed.

"Isn't this ever going to end?" Candy asked to no one in particular.

Bennett and Steven ran inside the hospital, Steven leading the way. They didn't stop until they'd reached Jeremy's room. When Steven saw Kathryn, he smiled; she was safe.

"Christopher took some men over to your house, Jeremy," Bennett said as he closed the door behind him. He held his gun at the ready while Steven went to stand by the window. "If Douglas went there, they should be able to catch him." No one said anything else for quite a while. People had already been cleared out of the hallways of the hospital, just in case. Jeremy closed his eyes as pain began to replace fear.

"Jeremy?" Candy asked softly.

"I'm all right, don't worry," he replied, opening his eyes. Kathryn went over to the deputy and spoke quietly.

"Uncle Ed, I think my father needs the doctor," she said. Bennett looked past her to where Jeremy lay and nodded.

"I'll get her," he said. "You lock this door behind me." Kathryn nodded and did so.

A few moments later, she opened the door only after Bennett let her know it was him. He and Dr. Wright came inside then he closed and locked the door again. Allyn went to check on Jeremy, who protested that he was okay.

"I'm just tired," he said.

"Yes, I'm sure you are," she replied but checked his wounds anyway. "Candy, would you get me some clean bandages out of the cabinet over there?" she asked.

"Of course," Candy said and was soon back with the requested items. She assisted the doctor and was relieved to see how much Jeremy's wounds had healed.

"The body's pretty amazing, isn't it?" Allyn asked her and smiled.

"Yes."

"Now then, I'm going to give you some laudanum, no protests," Allyn told Jeremy.

"No," he said as he looked her in the eye. He was hurting some, but he could handle it for a while, he thought. "When this is over."

"Jeremy..."

"No, Doctor. If...if something should happen, I might need to get out of here. I'd just be deadweight if I was asleep. If it hurts too much, believe me, I'll let you know."

"All right," she agreed and Jeremy sighed.

About an hour later, someone knocked at the door. Bennett brought his gun up to eye level and looked around the room before saying anything. Jason, Joshua, and Steven all stood in front of the bed and the women. Bennett focused his attention back on the person at the door.

"It's Chris Pruitt!" came Christopher's welcome voice. Bennett cracked the door open and, seeing Christopher, opened it all the way.

"You find him?" Bennett asked.

"Yep. It's over. We turned Douglas over to your deputies at the jail," Chris replied, looking pretty proud. "And the marshal's deputies are here, too. They brought one of those wagons, you know—looks like a jail on wheels."

"Good. Where'd you catch him?"

"At Jeremy's house."

"Good work, Chris; I'd better get right over there...sign Douglas and the others over," Bennett said and left.

"I'm glad that's over," Kathryn exclaimed.

"Well, he wouldn't have been successful this time," Steven said, putting an arm around his fiancée.

"Thanks, Chris; thanks a lot," Jeremy said with a deep sigh. "Look, I hate to spoil the party but I'm feeling real tired now."

"Of course. You get some rest," Jason stated. "We'll be back to see you in the morning."

Everyone but Candy left at that. She pulled her chair closer to the bed and Jeremy couldn't help but shake his head and smile. A low moan escaped his lips and he felt his wife's hand on his.

"I'm sure Dr. Wright will be back in soon," Candy said softly.

"Good. I'm glad it's all over...finally," Jeremy said and closed his fingers around Candy's.

"Thank God no one else was injured. And you'll soon be well enough to go home."

"It'll be awhile before things are back to normal, though. Candy?"

"Hmmm?"

"How bad does Seattle look?"

"I want to cry every time I have to see it," she replied honestly.

"That bad? I guess I knew it had to be, though. Did the

hotel burn down?"

"It was...how did Jason put it...gutted. The outside walls are still up, but there's not much left inside."

"Well, I hope people rebuild soon." Jeremy closed his eyes and only reopened them when he heard the doctor come inside.

"How's the pain?" she asked.

"Get right to it, don't you?" he asked, grinning. "Pretty bad, actually."

"You're getting too good at not showing it," Candy admonished.

"No point in worrying you," he replied with a sigh. To his surprise, Dr. Wright injected a hypodermic. He sighed again as the throbbing in his chest and shoulder slowly disappeared. "How come the shot?" he asked.

"Works faster. And I want you to sleep."

"I will. Thanks."

"You staying with him?" Allyn asked Candy.

"Yes."

"You...you should go home, Candy," Jeremy said as he slowly opened and closed his eyes. "You need some rest, too."

"I will, don't worry. You just do what the doctors say."

"Yes, ma'am."

"I like a man who knows his place," Allyn quipped with a laugh.

"I..." Jeremy's weary voice trailed off as he breathed deeply and his eyes closed again.

"He's asleep, Candy," Allyn said quietly. "He's right, though. You should go home. We'll take good care of him."

"I'll stay for just a while," Candy said firmly. No one was running her out until she was ready. Allyn nodded and left the room.

Two days later, Dr. Wright was getting ready to go home for the day. She decided to go in and check on Jeremy before leaving. When she walked into his room, she was stunned by what she saw.

"And just what do you think you're doing?" she asked sternly.

"Gettin' outta here," he replied matter-of-factly. He was trying to get dressed, but it was slow-going. A sudden pain forced him to sit back down. "In...a...minute."

"Listen, I'll let you go home, all right? But let me give you something for that pain and I'll send for someone to take you home. All right?"

"All right," he sighed but grinned. "Thanks." Allyn smiled and shook her head. She left for only a few moments. When she returned, Jeremy had managed to pull his pants on. She poured into a spoon some medicine which he gratefully swallowed.

"Now, I want you to lie back down until someone gets here," the doctor instructed. "You'll feel drowsy from the laudanum anyway. No walking around, all right?"

"Deal."

"And I'll be around this evening to check on you, so I expect to see you in your bed at home. Understood?"

"No argument." Jeremy lay back and closed his eyes. Allyn knew he'd probably go to sleep. She smiled and went to make all the release arrangements.

Chapter Sixteen

Mayor Roberts looked out over a crowd of people gathered in Seattle's town square. The old totem pole still stood, a symbol of Seattle's beginnings. The mayor waited until the people quieted down before speaking.

"Citizens of Seattle!" he said loudly. "We have two choices facing us!"

"Oh hell, Mayor, we got *one* choice! And that's to rebuild!" one man yelled. People started clapping in agreement, silencing the mayor. Martin Roberts held up his hands as he patiently waited. He was a politician, through and through, but a rarity in his field; most people felt he could be trusted. And being a single man with some attractive attributes made him a hit with the ladies. One of the ladies' groups was constantly after him to decide on a wife and he knew he'd eventually have to do that. Keeping his political career alive would depend, in part, on having a stable family life.

Jason Bolt stepped up and the crowd almost immediately quieted. Roberts shook his head; why Jason had never run for political office was beyond him. Jason's silver tongue could persuade almost anyone about practically anything. The mayor even envied Jason's gift of the language and his natural charisma.

"Now that that's settled," Jason boomed, "we need to think about how we're going to do that."

"Brick and stone!" Stempel shouted. "We've got to make sure we don't get wiped out again, even if another fire hits us."

"Stempel's right," Joshua agreed.

"What about the water line, Stempel?" someone yelled.

"It'll be completely finished this time," the sawmill owner promised.

"Aaron Stempel is not to blame for that," Roberts said. "I have the proof in my office if anyone cares to look at it."

"Thanks, Martin," Stempel said quietly, grinning.

People started talking amongst themselves; they'd decided. A real spirit lived in each and every person gathered— a strong will to overcome the most severe of catastrophes. What would come to be known as "the Seattle Spirit" had been born.

Joshua opened his mouth to speak again when he stopped. He smiled as Jeremy slowly walked up to where his brothers stood, aided by his daughter. Kathryn kept pushing a cane at her father, and he kept waving it away.

"I don't need it," he whispered.

"Yes, you do," she whispered back. "I'll tell Dr. Wright!"

"You wouldn't."

"I think I'd do as I was told," Joshua said with a laugh.

"I don't need it," Jeremy sighed but took the cane from Kathryn. Not being able to use his right arm much yet, it was awkward to handle the cane with his left. "See?" he said.

"You'll get used to it," Kathryn stated, a smug smile crossing her face. She clasped her hands in front of her, rocking back on her heels...she had won.

"No, I won't." Jeremy was practically pouting. "I mean, it's not like I have a broken leg or anything."

"Jeremy, good to see you up and around," Stempel said, rescuing him. "Why don't you take a seat up here?"

"Thanks, Aaron," he replied and shot his daughter a nasty smile.

"I'll tell," she warned then laughed. Candy had told her to keep her father in line. Kathryn intended to do just that. "I have my orders from Mother," she added and Jeremy rolled his eyes and groaned.

"Women!" he exclaimed.

"Remember, it was you men who gave us the vote," Kathryn said, crossing her arms. "And it was you Bolts who brought Seattle a woman doctor. And it was—"

"Yeah, yeah, we know," Joshua stated then laughed. "Heaven help us...you're just like Candy."

Jeremy's blue eyes twinkled as he chuckled. "Isn't that the truth?" he agreed. "I'll be careful, I promise," he told his daughter.

"Promise?" she asked.

"I said I would, didn't I?" His voice leveled and Kathryn caught the warning. He turned to the other men. "Now, what have I missed?"

"We were just talking about rebuilding," Joshua said. "You know, some of these people aren't going to be able to afford the right materials."

"Then we've got to pool our resources," Jason said. He turned back to the crowd. "We need to get estimates on the damages first," he shouted. "When that's done, those who need help with finances, come see the Bolt brothers." That said, he looked at his brothers and hunched his shoulders. There was a low murmuring of voices as people talked amongst themselves again. A few men came up to Jason, the general store owner Ben Perkins among them.

"I hate to ask you boys for a loan, but..." he began.

"I know, Ben, I know," Jason said quietly. "How're Emily

and the family?"

"Taking it pretty well. Thanks, Jason." He and Jason shook hands then Ben left.

"Well, guess the hard part's over," Joshua surmised.

"What do you mean, Uncle Josh?" Kathryn asked.

"Folks have accepted the fact that the fire happened. Now, they're ready to rebuild and get Seattle back up." Jeremy stood up, took his cane, and started to walk away. Joshua cleared his throat and put a hand on Jeremy's shoulder. "Just where do you think you're going?"

"I'll...see ya later," Jeremy said.

"Oh no, you don't, little brother. There's a lot to do and if you can be on your feet..."

"I've still gotta take it easy," he said in mock protest. "I'm not a well man...the doc says..." he chuckled and, of course, stayed put. Jason put out his hand, Joshua placed his on top, then Jeremy added his. Jason sealed the clasp with his other hand—the old Bolt pledge.

"What a group I'm related to," Kathryn said with a laugh.

By morning, tents stood next to charred buildings in the city. It was business as usual for most of the town's merchants. People just coming into town were amazed at the vast array of businesses still in operation.

At Jeremy's house, the pace was a bit more relaxed. Jeremy lay in bed, watching Candy dress for the day. He gently ran his hand across the bandage on his chest and sighed.

"Why don't you stay in bed today?" Candy suggested.

"Sounds like a good idea," he said. "But Jason and Josh need me. Besides, Dr. Wright thinks I can be up for a little while longer each day. And I do like to be outdoors. Don't worry, I'll be careful...I'll act as foreman. Boss my brothers around." He chuckled at that and Candy shook her head and smiled.

"Need some help?" she asked when Jeremy sat up very slowly.

"I...think I can manage," he replied, reaching for the

clothing Candy had laid out for him. "It's amazing how much we take for granted. So, what are your plans today?" He stood up and pulled his pants on, then reached for his shirt.

"Cooking mostly. Some of the other women are gathering meals to take to town."

"Guess I'll be downtown, too. Stempel's house survived, I hear. Pretty clever strategy he had." He looked around the room. "Where are my boots?"

"Wherever you took them off, I expect," Candy said absently.

"Candy, you know—"

"I know, your memory isn't what it used to be," she interrupted, laughing.

"I've got an excuse, you know," he complained. "It's hard to remember my name, let alone anything else."

"Jeremy Bolt!" Candy supplied. "You shouldn't blame that for your poor memory. You were forgetful before you were..." She didn't—couldn't—finish. The shooting was still something she had a hard time talking about. She was grateful she still had Jeremy.

"Ha! Ha!" Jeremy sneered at her, trying to lighten the situation. "Don't worry, I'll find 'em myself!" Candy turned to go when Jeremy grabbed her from behind. As his lips covered hers, she still managed to speak.

"Thought...you weren't...a well man," she murmured but closed her eyes and put her arms around her husband. She wanted to hold him tight but knew she couldn't yet. His kiss let her know he felt the same desire as she.

"Well, looks like Dad is back to normal," Jonathan announced as he came bursting into the room.

"Jonathan!" Candy exclaimed, embarrassed.

"Looks like we're caught," Jeremy laughed, his left arm still around his wife. His face glowed as red as hers. Kathryn poked her head in and smiled.

"Oh, Jonathan, leave 'em alone!" she said. "It's good to see them like this again."

"It's embarrassin'," the ten-year-old whined. He ran out,

headed for the kitchen, and yelled back, "What's for breakfast?"

"Guess things *are* back to normal," Jeremy quipped but gave Candy another kiss before releasing her. He went off in search of his boots while Candy and Kathryn headed for the kitchen.

Kathryn slowly urged her horse along what the loggers called Skid Road a couple of days later. The road was extremely bumpy as small logs were buried about halfway into the ground, spaced several feet apart. In order to get the logs to the waterfront, one man would grease the skids while others controlled horses or oxen pulling loads of logs down along the road.

With recovery efforts underway on a grand scale, not much logging was being done on Bridal Veil Mountain. Kathryn had chosen to travel down the main skid road because it was a much shorter way into Seattle. She felt she had waited long enough.

As she rode into town, she spotted her father and his brothers talking with Steven. She rode on toward them and Jeremy greeted her first.

"What are you doing down here so early?" he asked.

"I came to see my future husband," she said. Steven smiled at her but she did not return the sentiment as she slid off her horse. Taking Steven's hand, she turned to the Bolt brothers, who were grinning. "I need to talk to Steven alone," she said. "I'm sure you'll get along without him?" She did not wait around for a reply and Steven couldn't hide an amused smile, although he managed to hold in his laughter.

Laughter was something the Bolts did *not* try to hide. Joshua went up to Jeremy and patted his left arm.

"Doesn't she remind you of someone, Jeremy?" he asked.

"Too much sometimes. But, if she weren't like her mother, I'd probably worry," Jeremy replied with a chuckle.

"Poor Steven," Jason howled.

Several hundred feet away, Kathryn finally stopped in front of a newly laid foundation. Steven was silent as he waited to see what was on her mind. He knew better than to hazard a guess.

"So, what's on your mind?" he finally asked.

"I think it's time we made the trip down the aisle," she said seriously. "Or have you decided not to get married?"

"I was just waiting for…," Steven stammered.

"Yes? Waiting for?" Her arms were crossed and she impatiently tapped one foot.

"The right time. Look, Katy, I love you and I do want us to be married. But I just had to get my business going again. It took almost every cent I had to get started in the first place."

"Steven." Her tone softened and she smiled. "Let me help you rebuild. I'm part of your life and I want to be there to help. Besides, I'm a great carpenter! Just ask my father and uncles."

"All right," Steven laughed. "I guess Jeremy is well enough now, huh? When do you want to have the wedding?"

"Sunday."

"As in two days from now, Sunday? Are you serious?" he asked, startled.

"Quite serious. Can you be ready?" Kathryn laughed at her fiancé's panicked expression. He smiled again and took her in his arms.

"Your father warned me about you."

"Did he now? And just what did he say?"

"That you were headstrong, like your mother."

"I'll have to tell her," she threatened. "She'll tell you I'm a lot like my father."

"Listen, Sunday's just fine with me," Steven said quietly. "I'll find a suit somewhere."

"I'm sure one of the men in my family can produce something decent."

"Not going to let me wear my dungarees, huh? I think we'd better get back to the others. They might think we've decided to elope."

"Now there's an idea!" They both laughed at that and headed back toward the Bolt brothers.

Chapter Seventeen

Late the next morning, Kathryn urged her horse up the steep hill to her Uncle Jason's house. He was busy in town with the rebuilding efforts, but his niece knew that Roland Francis Clancey had remained indoors. In fact, he hadn't ventured outside since he'd lost his beloved old ship.

The front door stood open, as if beckoning her inside, so Kathryn did just that. It didn't take her long to find where the sea captain was. He sat on the big, overstuffed sofa in the drawing room, staring out a huge bay window. The view it provided was breathtaking—beautiful Lake Washington could be seen shimmering several hundred feet below.

"Lottie would say this view is wasted on you," Kathryn said softly, startling Clancey for just a moment.

"Aye, she would," he agreed and smiled.

"I'm sorry about your boat…ship. I know how much it meant to you."

"You know, dearie, when the *Shamus O'Flynn* went down in t'at harbor, I t'ought, 'There goes me life.' But I was wrong. I never had a family—real family—until I hooked up with the Bolt brothers."

"Can't seem to get rid of 'em, huh?" Kathryn asked with a laugh. She sat down next to Clancey. There was an empty whiskey bottle on the floor but Clancey did not smell of alcohol, surprising Kathryn.

"Don't think I haven't tried a time or two!" he said. "I'm all right though. I just needed some time to meself. Sort of a mournin' period, yas might say."

"Well then, we should have a wake for the old girl."

"You're right, darlin'! Are yas sure t'ere's not a wee bit o' Irish in yas?" He laughed and stood up, then planted his old, worn-out skipper's cap on his white head. "C'mon, darlin'! We're gonna give the ol' girl a proper good-bye!"

"I think everyone will be surprised," Kathryn said as she followed Clancey.

"Speaking of everyone," he said as his tone softened to one of concern, "how's Jeremy? Sorry I haven't been to see him."

"He'd have you believin' he's ship-shape! He's definitely much better, but Mother watches him. Dr. Wright is almost as bad as Mother. But Dad *is* taking it easier than he normally would." She paused and her eyes glimmered for just a moment. "He still has pain from time to time and I know that it frustrates him to not be active all the time."

"Well, your father always was one to go at life full bore. Especially when he was about your age."

"I love hearing everyone's stories about Mom and Dad. Jonathan gets embarrassed. Says he doesn't understand all that romancin' and stuff." Kathryn laughed and patted Clancey's shoulder. "Well, let's go get everybody together for this wake."

By dusk, the Bolt families, Clancey, Stempel, Biddie and Corky and their daughter, Melissa, Big Swede and Essie and

Peter, and some of the original brides and their families gathered around the spot where the *Shamus O'Flynn* had sunk. No one spoke for a while; sadness pervaded the group. Not even two of Seattle's best orators, Jason and Stempel, quite knew what to say yet.

The "old tub" held a lot of memories; it had brought one hundred young women to the Northwest wilderness long ago, and the dream that was Seattle had become a reality. And *that* was something to celebrate.

"Me ship lies silent and still but now is a time for celebratin' her history," Clancey said sadly.

"Clancey's right," Candy stated. "We should always have fond remembrances of the boat."

"Ah, Jason, will theys never learn?" Clancey wailed in mock despair. "It's a ship!" Everyone laughed knowingly.

"To the *Shamus O'Flynn*!" Jeremy shouted. "There may be a fleet of ships in and out of Seattle now, but one ol' mule scow started it all."

"Here, here!" Joshua said loudly.

"And now, me dear friends, a special toast. To Kathryn, who used to play on me ol' tub. May your life with Steven be filled with laughter."

"Thank you, Clancey," Kathryn said, embracing the old salt. "I have a toast for you, too. If Dad and his brothers hadn't hired you and your ship, I wouldn't be here."

"That's right. Clancey and his ship were sort of matchmakers," Joshua said, grinning.

"T'at and a six-month voyage!" Clancey bellowed and the others laughed, agreeing. "Thank you, all of yas. I once said that Jason Bolt could outsmart the devil himself, and I was right." Jason just shook his head as laughter permeated the group again. "He hornswoggled me into staying in Seattle all t'em year ago, but...I'm glad he did.

"And now, me dear friends, we should remember one other ol' girl—the one person who kept us all goin' t'rough thick and thin. Carlotta Hatfield." He doffed his worn-out cap and placed it over his heart. The women all smiled and tried to keep from crying.

"To Lottie!" they shouted.

"To Lottie!" everyone else chorused. Then, all fell silent for several minutes. Lottie had been there for all of them at some point or another.

Jeremy's memories of his youth came flooding back with a mixture of emotions. Although he continued to smile, his brow creased in almost a frown. Lottie had also helped the Bolt brothers bury their parents.

The sky seemed to grieve along with the tiny group of people huddled around a new gravesite as the gray clouds released a gentle shower. A plain pine coffin, adorned with wildflowers, was slowly lowered into its final resting place.

Jonathan Bolt and his three sons looked sadly on but no tears were evident. The minister slowly closed his Bible after he completed the somber service.

"Jonathan, is there anything more you'd like to say about your wife?" he asked.

"Father, I've written a prayer for Mother," a sixteen-year-old Jason said. "May I say it now?"

"Of course," his father replied. Jonathan placed a gentle hand on his eldest son's shoulder. Jason had grown up fast, his father realized. He was like Jonathan in so many ways, including being almost a spitting image of his father. At sixteen, Jason was already a man.

As Jason slowly read his prayer, Joshua, eleven years old, put his arm around his seven-year-old brother, Jeremy, who had started to cry again; Jeremy had been the closest to their mother.

"Amen," Jason ended his tribute to his mother as tears rolled silently down his face.

"Amen," Jonathan echoed.

"Amen," Joshua whispered.

"A-A-Am-m-m..." Jeremy stuttered, suddenly unable to say the word; his sobs strengthened. Jonathan quickly kneeled next to his little boy and hugged him.

"Shhh...it's all right, Jeremy," he whispered. "You don't have to say anything."

"B-But I w-w-want," Jeremy tried again and cried so hard, his father thought he might collapse. Jonathan easily scooped his youngest son into his arms and motioned to his other sons to follow. He knew that Jeremy would feel his mother's loss the most.

They quietly walked past the solitary grave marker that read simply, "Amanda Bolt, Beloved Wife and Mother." The untimely passing of his mother would mark the beginning of a long and difficult youth for Jeremy.

Jeremy was unaware of those around him for the moment as he remembered his mother's funeral. Tears misted in his eyes as he stared at the ground.

"Mom," he whispered.

Candy nudged her husband. He'd been silent a long time and the tears in his eyes told her he was remembering someone other than Lottie.

"What?" he asked absently. He looked up at his wife then cleared his throat. "Did you say something?"

"Are you all right?" she asked, worried. "Are you hurting?"

"No, I'm fine, really. I was just-just thinkin', but," he paused as he smiled again, "it's not important now. Have I missed something?"

"No, nothing."

"Well, it's gettin' late," Jason stated. "It's good to remember and we shall all have wonderful memories of the ship and all she represented. She brought the brides to Seattle, Clancey found a home. And, Lottie, dear Lottie, held us all together.

"But now we have new memories to make. Kathryn and Steven will be married Sunday, and, God willing, another generation will bless Seattle."

"Jason, I'm not ready to be a grandfather yet," Jeremy said woefully. "Don't be in such a hurry!" Then he laughed along with the others.

"Jason's right," Clancey spoke up, putting his cap back on. "The time to say good-bye is over. Good night is what we should be sayin' now." Hugs were exchanged as the small gathering of people slowly broke up. They had gone through a lot to build their lives, and with hard work, they'd rebuild their city. Kathryn and Steven's wedding would be the first marriage of the new beginning.

Jason awoke at dawn to the sound of the front door opening and shutting. He got up, knowing it was too early for Mrs. Wong, his housekeeper, to be in yet.

"Clancey," Jason spoke to thin air. He donned his pants and walked out to the drawing room just in time to see Clancey through the window. He was headed down the hill toward the lake. Jason sighed, knowing instantly where Clancey was going.

Clancey wiped the morning dew off a gray tombstone and smiled sadly. "Carlotta Hatfield" was the only writing inscribed on the granite. Clancey sat down on a bench he'd placed beside the grave so many years ago.

"Oh Lottie, me girl," he said quietly as if he knew she could hear, "we sure coulda used yas these last few days. I'm sure you've seen what's happening to Seattle. 'Tis a shame, it is. Jeremy was hurt, real bad, for a time, but he's gonna be all right. I knew you'd want to know that. I know how you loved them, those Bolt brothers. Aye, and t'ey loved yas, too.

"I know you'd be proud of how folks's been gettin' along, though. There's a real strong spirit to t'ese people. But you knew that, too." He sighed and wiped a solitary tear away. "Me old tub is gone, though. Down to the dark depths, she is.

"We had us some fine times, didn't we, ol' girl?" He sighed again and closed his eyes.

A thick layer of white had blanketed almost every inch of Seattle, and the snow continued to fall. Townspeople were afraid if it kept up, they'd be isolated from the outside world. It had been many years since Seattle had been so deeply covered in white.

Lottie Hatfield, owner of Lottie's Saloon and Boarding House, peered out the window at the snow. She pulled her woolen shawl tighter around her and turned back to her employee.

"It's really comin' down out there. Brrr! Gettin' real cold, too."

"Are you all right, Lottie?" Ken, her bartender and all-around helper, asked.

"Oh sure, Ken. You ought to go on home. We can finish that inventory another time. With the snow coming down this heavy, I'm not sure we'll have any customers tonight anyway, except maybe Clancey." They both laughed at that. It would take a lot to keep that seaman out of the saloon.

"You go on now," Lottie urged. "Your wife will be worried about you making it home in this."

"All right," Ken replied, putting on his coat and scarf, "if you're sure you're okay."

"Go on, get! I'm just gonna go in the parlor and stoke my fire. Maybe I'll read for a bit. You know, Christopher Pruitt brought over one of those mystery books he likes the other day. I haven't decided if I really like them or not yet. He says it's the latest thing to read." Ken nodded and went out the door. Lottie locked up and went into the back parlor. She wasn't all right; she was ill again, and she knew it.

Ken reigned his horse up short in front of Joshua Bolt's house and dismounted. He pounded on the door, even though he knew Joshua would be home. There had been no logging for two days now.

Joshua opened the door and invited Ken inside, although the fair-haired Bolt was surprised. Ken followed his host into the kitchen where Callie and Jason were. Callie offered him a cup of coffee, which he gratefully accepted.

"Jason, Joshua, I only stopped by because I'm really worried about Lottie," Ken said.

"Is she ill again?" Callie asked.

"I think so. She hasn't complained of anything in particular, but I do think she's sick."

"The doctor just saw Lottie a week ago, Ken," Jason said. "She said Lottie was just fine."

"Yeah, I know that but, well, I just can't explain it, Jason. I mean, I work with Lottie on a daily basis. I would just feel better if you'd look in on her later…just to make sure she's all right. She'd admit how she's feeling to you."

"Of course we will, Ken," Joshua assured the man. "Would you stop by Jeremy's and ask him to come down?"

"Sure. Thanks." Ken took his leave as Jason, Joshua, and Callie talked quietly about the many bouts with illness Lottie had had over the years. She was getting on in years, after all.

Not long after, all three Bolt brothers arrived at Lottie's and hastened to dismount. Jason pounded on the door but received no answer. Pulling his coat tighter around him, he pounded again. When he still heard nothing, he backed up just slightly and kicked the door in. Joshua and Jeremy followed close behind, thankful to get in out of the biting snow.

"C'mon, boys, one of you check upstairs, and the other the back," Jason said authoritatively. "I'll check out the storeroom."

"Good thing Ken stopped by, huh?" Joshua asked and the three split up. Jeremy rushed into the back parlor and found Lottie lying on the floor, a blanket still wrapped around her. He knelt beside her and heaved a sigh of relief upon finding a pulse. She was alive but burning up with fever.

"Jason! Josh! Hurry!" Jeremy yelled, afraid to move from Lottie's side. His brothers came running in and Jason bent down to check their friend as well.

"Jeremy, go get the doctor and I'll take Lottie upstairs to her room."

"On my way," Jeremy said and was out the door. He trudged through the calf-deep snow, keeping his head down. Ice mixed in with the wet snow and made the short distance to the medical clinic seem much longer. Jeremy knew Dr. Wright would be in…she was always in.

When he got to the clinic door, he could see that he was right. A light glowed through the window and he tried to open the door but found it locked. He knocked loudly, yelling as he did so.

"Dr. Wright! Open up!"

"Jeremy, what on earth?" the doctor asked, seeing Jeremy standing outside. "Come in, come in," she added, ushering him inside.

"It's L-Lottie," he said, wiping his face with the cloth she handed him. "She's real sick."

"What happened?" she asked as she quickly gathered items for her medical bag.

"I don't know. But she's burning up with a fever. When we found her, she was unconscious."

"She seemed fine the last time I examined her."

"Please hurry, D-Doc!" Jeremy pleaded and grabbed the doctor's bag while she put her coat and boots on.

"I'm ready," she said, patting his arm. "Let's go."

A couple of hours later, Allyn Wright slowly descended the stairs to the main saloon. She noted that Clancey had gotten there; *Jason Bolt is a smart man*, she thought. He knew that the sea captain loved Lottie Hatfield although the two had remained only friends throughout their relationship.

"How is she, Doctor?" Clancey asked first.

"She's failing fast," Allyn said sadly, her hand resting on the railing. "I'm afraid there's nothing I can do. The pneumonia is beyond my help."

"Are you…are you sure?" Joshua asked, unable to believe it.

"I'm sure, Joshua. I'm really sorry. She's resting as comfortably as can be expected. You can go in, one at a time, to see her…but only for a minute." The doctor paused and looked into the saddened faces of Lottie's friends. She softly added, "She knows. I think she's known all along."

Clancey reluctantly opened his eyes with a sigh. He leaned over and gently ran a shaky hand across the top of the tombstone.

"Ah, Lottie darlin', I shoulda asked yas to marry me. I'm

not sure you would have, but I wish I'd at least asked yas."

"She might have surprised you," Jason said, startling Clancey. "Mind if I join you?" Clancey smiled and motioned for Jason to sit down. Jason took in a deep breath then put an arm around his old friend. "It's pretty here, isn't it?" he asked.

"Aye. She liked it up here. It's where she came to think things out, she used to say. Said you told her about it. Now, she's got it all to herself. A little selfish of her, wouldn't yas say?"

"A bit," Jason said and chuckled. "I think she's entitled. Well, guess I'll head on into town, see how things are going. Coming?"

"Nah, not yet, bucko. You go on. I'll be all right."

"All right. I'll see you later." Jason patted Clancey's shoulder as he stood up.

Chapter Eighteen

Jeremy was very still as Dr. Wright examined him. He had done all that she had advised but it still seemed to be taking forever to recover.

"Well, I wouldn't try dancing a jig just yet, and I don't want you trotting around on that jittery horse of yours. Your wounds are healing well," Allyn Wright stated firmly as she replaced the bandage on his chest. "Candy must be keeping you in line."

"That she is," Jeremy confirmed with a laugh.

"I want you to keep the bandages on a few more days."

"All right. Candy helps me change them but I think it bothers her to look."

"She still won't talk about the shooting?"

"Nope."

"Well, you were very lucky."

"I know," Jeremy replied soberly as he sat up. "Finished?"

"Yes. You can button up now." Jeremy did so as Dr. Wright cleared away the old bandages. "The bandages are more of a precaution than anything. I don't want to risk infection." Jeremy nodded and stood up, wincing as he did so.

"Gettin' old sure has its drawbacks," he said with a grin.

"Sometimes," Allyn agreed, smiling. "Are you still having a lot of pain?"

"No. Just got a little stiff laying down for so long." He slipped his right arm back inside its sling. "How much longer do I need to use this?"

"Maybe another week." She paused and eyed him curiously. "You haven't been using it much, have you?"

"Uh, well..." Jeremy knew he'd been caught. "Not much. But-but my shoulder feels fine. It gets stiff if I don't use it."

"I understand. But use the sling, all right? Just to be on the safe side."

"All right."

"How much physical work are you actually doing?"

"Honestly? None," Jeremy sighed. "I'm...overseeing things. No one will even let me near a hammer. My wife, my brothers, even my children!"

"Well, good for them," Allyn said, laughing. Jeremy grinned and nodded.

"I figured you'd enjoy hearing that."

"So, how're the wedding plans coming?"

"Ask Candy! I'm stayin' out of it this time."

"Might be the wisest thing."

"Yeah. Well, thanks, Doc." Jeremy started to leave then turned back to the doctor. "See ya at the wedding?"

"Wouldn't miss it," she replied.

Jason and several others were gathered in front of Perkins' General Store, near Seattle's main waterfront district. The new structure was almost finished. Ben Perkins stepped back to watch as the sign was being attached.

"Well, Ben, looks as if we've got our general store back,"

Jason said as he clapped his friend on the back.

"Thanks, Jason. As soon as we're up and runnin' again, you and your brothers will be repaid. You can bet on it."

"Thought your bettin' days were over, Ben!" Joshua said with a laugh.

"Only when I'm around Emily!" Ben retorted. He looked around and noticed that someone was missing. "Jeremy taking it easy for a change?" he asked.

"Are you serious?" Joshua asked, grinning. "He's over at the hospital, getting a check up. I'm sure you'll see him around later."

"Unless Dr. Wright ties him up," said Jason.

"Oh, she wouldn't do that," Biddie said, shaking her head. She looked thoughtful for a moment, then added, "On the other hand, maybe she would." She laughed and got the others started. When Biddie started her unusual laughter, it was contagious.

Jason and Joshua mounted their horses, continuing their tour of the reconstruction efforts. Tents were set up near each business construction site. Business as usual, they noted, despite all that had happened. The two brothers exchanged smiles then turned in the direction of the city's jail. Ed Bennett would be waiting to see them.

Bennett sat quietly at his desk, struggling with his report. So much had happened in such a short period of time, he hadn't kept up with the paperwork. His wife, Molly, usually handled that for him. She was Candy's sister and had had to return to New Bedford, Massachusetts, to take care of the Pruitt family holdings. Candy had been too busy with her civic duties to go, but Molly hadn't made the journey east in several years and had been delighted to make the trip. Their brother, Christopher, had accompanied her, but as soon as news of the fire had reached them, he turned back. With Molly being such a seasoned traveler, Christopher had felt it safe for her to continue on to New Bedford alone.

Bennett looked up as Jason and Joshua Bolt and Aaron Stempel walked inside. He nodded and motioned for them to take a seat. Grateful for the reprieve from writing, he pushed the paperwork aside.

"Thanks for coming," he said. "I just wanted to speak to you about this man you brought in the other night. He's not in very good shape, mentally, I mean. I don't think he has any family. Dr. Michaels spent some time with him. We can't get any information on who he is other than the name Willie."

"So, what are you proposing?" Jason asked.

"Having him institutionalized. There's a pretty good asylum in Olympia. Dr. Michaels has already written a letter for commitment."

"What about the fires?" Stempel asked.

"Like I told you before, you'd be surprised what people like him are capable of. He sits back there in his cell and laughs about blowing Seattle off the map."

"There's probably no way we'll ever know for sure, is there?" Joshua asked. "I mean, Jerome Douglas refused to confess to setting any fire."

"Probably not, but with Jeremy charging him with attempted murder, Douglas will be tried for that. He's been charged with arson as well but I don't think that'll stick if he continuously refuses to admit to it." Bennett heaved a sigh and added, "And, he may be innocent of that anyway."

"You might be right," Jason said. "It might have just been a convenient coincidence. The fire certainly afforded him the opportunity to come and go at will."

"Well, almost at will," said Aaron.

"You're right, Aaron," Joshua said, nodding.

"Jeremy ever say why Douglas even showed up in Seattle?" Bennett asked.

"Jealousy," Jason replied with a shrug. "Kathryn basically turned down his affections. I suppose rejection can get the better of some people."

"Yeah," Joshua muttered. "And it almost got Jeremy killed."

"He's certainly hard to keep down, though," Bennett said, grinning. "I've seen him ordering you two around."

"Yeah," Jason said, standing. "I'll be glad when he's completely recovered." All four men laughed heartily at that.

"Well, I'd better take off," Joshua said, standing. "I'll see you at Jeremy's tonight. You coming, Ed?"

"If I can. Depends on this damnable paperwork! I'll be glad when Molly gets back!"

"Try to make it," Jason said. He turned to Joshua. "See you there." Joshua nodded and left. Jason and Aaron left soon after.

Early that evening, Jeremy stepped out onto his front porch and slowly breathed in the night air. He leaned over the railing and gazed at the lights in the town below. Voices of the others inside could still be heard but Jeremy paid no attention to them.

Kathryn quietly stood in the open door and smiled. She had seen her father leave the festivities inside, and it worried her a bit. His health had improved at a rapid pace but she knew he was far from being completely well. Her mother had told her that much.

"Are you all right, Daddy?" she asked as she joined him. He did not turn to her as he spoke.

"I'm fine. Just…remembering."

"A lot has changed, hasn't it?"

"Hmmm?" Jeremy asked absently.

"Thank you, Daddy," Kathryn said and hugged her father, surprising him.

"You're welcome, I think. What did I do?"

"For…everything. For letting Steven come to dinner tonight. You broke with tradition, you know."

"Oh. Well, with all that's happened, I just thought tradition was out of place here." Jeremy sighed and finally got to the heart of what he was feeling. "It's…hard to see you leave."

"I've grown up, Dad."

"Yes, I've noticed." He smiled sadly.

"We didn't have this kind of conversation the first time. Why now?"

"Oh, I don't know. I guess because the only worry on our minds then was giving you a perfect wedding."

"Yeah. No fire...no Jerome Douglas." Kathryn shuddered at mentioning the name. Jeremy put an arm around her and nodded.

"Well, he's out of your life for good."

"I know. But it still scares me that you got hurt. It scares Mother, too."

"I've seen the worry in her eyes," Jeremy replied, sighing. "I feel guilty about it, too."

"Why?"

"Because I could have prevented what happened."

"How?"

"I knew Douglas was armed. When Josh left the hotel, I could have gone back with him to get a crew myself. I told your mother all that but—"

"But she argued the point with you," Kathryn interrupted and managed a smile.

"Right. Guess I'll never win." Jeremy chuckled. "You'd think I'd win one after all these years."

"I hope Steven and I are as happy as you and Mother," Kathryn said softly, wistfully.

"I hope you are, too. Just remember to listen to one another, every now and then. That's something your mother and I are still learning how to do." He started to say more when his wife came out. "How long have you been there?" he asked her.

"Long enough," Candy replied, trying to not smile.

"I'll see you two inside," Kathryn said, unable to hide an amused smile. "Steven will think I've deserted him."

"Well, got any more of that sage advice?" Candy asked after their daughter had gone back inside.

"Oh, I don't know. Maybe. You in need of some?"

"No. Just wondering." Candy sat down on the cushioned bench and Jeremy joined her.

"Remember how you volunteered me to go with Lottie up to help Bethany Albright?"

"Yes, why?"

"And remember how we argued about it?"

"Yes. And I remember telling you I'd help you get used to arguing with me."

"Yeah? How?" Jeremy's mouth curved upward into a mischievous grin. Candy took his face in her hands and brought him close for a kiss. Jeremy closed his eyes as he took her in his arms, prolonging the moment.

"Oh, not again!" Jonathan wailed, stepping outside.

"We're caught...again!" Jeremy said, clearing his throat. "Go on in, we'll be in soon," he told his son.

"Guess we better go in, huh?" Candy asked as she laid her head on her husband's shoulder.

"Yep. We'll have time for us later. Tonight belongs to our daughter." Jeremy smiled sadly. "Their life together certainly isn't starting out very easy."

"No, but it'll make them appreciate each other that much more. Look at us."

"Yeah. They'll do fine. C'mon, let's go inside."

A short time later, the Bolt families and close friends gathered around the dinner table. Mouth-watering smells permeated the room as they began to partake of the delicious meal. Candy had always been a wonderful cook and she'd successfully passed her skills on to her daughter.

"Well, Steven," Jason said, "looks like you won't starve."

"You're not wrong there," Steven agreed as he dug into his first bite of roast beef.

"Hey, I helped," Jonathan complained.

"Shhh," Jeremy whispered to his son.

"Well, I did!"

"Maybe one man in the family will learn how to cook," said Joshua.

"You and Jason usually made the food disappear," Jeremy said, sneering at his brother.

"We didn't have any other choice," Jason howled. "As bad as some of our meals were, you still cooked better than Josh or myself." Laughter erupted around the room but Jeremy chose to sulk.

"Excuse me," he said and pushed away from the table.

"Oh, come on, we're only joking," Joshua said, shaking his head.

"I know," Jeremy replied, unable to hide a grin. "I'll be right back." He chuckled as he headed for the kitchen. Candy frowned but said nothing. She hadn't forgotten to bring anything out.

Jeremy went through the kitchen and out of the house. He lit the wicks on the lights on both sides of the door. With a heavy sigh, he sat down in a chair. Perspiration had quickly formed on his face and his shirt was already sticking to him. The dull ache in his chest had been tolerable until now. He knew Dr. Wright had given Candy a bottle of laudanum for him but he didn't know where she'd put it, nor did he want to ask her. Not yet.

The warm night air seemed to help him and he leaned back. He'd just stay outside a few minutes, he thought. He closed his eyes and took slow, deep breaths.

Inside the house, Candy seemed to be the only person uncomfortable with Jeremy's absence. She had tried not to nag him when he was in pain, but it was hard for her. It was going to take a long time for him to get back to normal, and she knew it frustrated him.

"Mom, what's wrong?" Kathryn whispered to her mother.

"Nothing," Candy tried to be cheerful and smiled.

"I know that look. Is Dad okay?"

"Yes, I'm sure he is."

"You want me to go check on him, Candy?" Joshua asked and immediately everyone at the table stopped talking. Candy bit down on her lip then shook her head.

"No, I'll go. I wouldn't be surprised if Jeremy's cooking something; then he'll make Jason and Joshua eat it, just to get even!" she said with a sincere laugh. "Please, enjoy yourselves while I go rescue my kitchen." She got up, still smiling, and headed for the kitchen. Conversations picked up where they'd been left off and Candy was glad to hear the noise begin again.

The kitchen door was cracked just a bit and Candy saw the light from the porch. Nodding her head, she went up the stairs to her and Jeremy's bedroom. She knew her husband had gone outside for more than just a little fresh air.

"Hello," she greeted him. Jeremy sat up in his chair.

"Candy, um, uh, hello," he said and cleared his throat.

"I thought you could use some of this," she said as she produced a spoon and a bottle of medicine. Jeremy grinned and nodded. He gratefully swallowed the tasteless liquid and sighed as the laudanum sent a warming numbness through him.

"Thanks," he whispered and closed his eyes again. Candy sat beside him then.

"Better?"

"Much. Sorry." A frown creased his brow and he opened his eyes.

"Don't be. Kathryn will understand."

"Understand what?"

"Why you need to go to bed." Candy's voice was firm and authoritative. Jeremy chuckled and his blue eyes sparkled.

"I think I can handle being up for a while longer," he replied and took his wife's hand. "Besides, I don't want to ruin this night for her. As much as it hurts to see her go, it would make me feel that much worse if I spoiled things for her."

"I honestly don't think you could spoil anything for your daughter. She worships you."

"I'm...not so sure about that. She's been very bossy ever since I got shot."

"Well, we have to keep you in line," Candy quipped, but Jeremy saw the uneasy look that had crossed her face. He leaned over and brushed her lips with his.

"Someday, we're gonna have to talk about it, Candy," he said afterward. "I need to talk about it."

"All right."

"Now, what say we go back in and eat? I'm hungry now!" He stood and pulled at his shirt. "I think I'll go change this shirt first."

"I'll fix you a new plate. I'm sure your food is cold now."

"Thanks. I won't be long," he said. They touched hands for only a moment. Candy sighed and went back inside as well. She put the laudanum in a kitchen cabinet; she'd let Jeremy know where it was in case he needed it again.

"Well, what have I missed?" Jeremy asked as he sat back down at the table. No one asked any questions and he didn't offer any explanation for his absence. Candy put another plate of food in front of him and he nodded.

"Jason and I figured we were gonna get something else to eat," Joshua said with a laugh.

"I think my cookin' days are over," Jeremy replied between mouthsful.

"Oh, I don't know," Kathryn said, "you do real well with steaks."

"Thanks. I appreciate the support," Jeremy said, chuckling. A few minutes later, he pushed his plate away. He was starting to feel a little groggy but the food helped control that.

"Why don't we have coffee and cordials in the parlor?" Candy suggested. "You men go on in and we'll join you in just a bit."

Once the drinks had been served, Candy sat beside Jeremy. He took her hand then turned his attention to his daughter and Steven.

"Well, this is it...again!" he said quietly, smiling. "I wish you every happiness."

"Thank you, Jeremy," Steven said.

"I'd like to propose a toast," Jason said as he stood up. Everyone else followed suit and lifted their glasses. Jason was just about to continue when a knock sounded at the door.

"I'll get it, Mom," Jonathan called out as he ran to the door. "Mom! Dad!" he yelled and both Candy and Jeremy practically ran out.

"Oh, Molly!" Candy exclaimed and hugged her sister. Molly Bennett stood back after embracing Candy and smiled. Her blond hair hung in silky ringlets about her shoulders and it was Jeremy who noticed the change in her appearance first.

"You-You're pr-pr—," he stuttered but Molly interrupted him.

"Yes, I'm pregnant," she said, smiling at her brother-in-law. "Don't I get a hug from you, too?" she asked and Jeremy nodded, smiling. The embrace was very brief and Molly looked at him in wonder. Jeremy was usually a little more affectionate than that, she knew. She noticed that his right arm was in a sling.

"Come on inside," Candy said and took Molly's hand. They walked into the parlor where hugs and kisses were exchanged.

"I'm so glad you're back," Kathryn said. "Our wedding is tomorrow."

"Oh, good! I figured I'd missed it."

"Why didn't you go to New Bedford?" Joshua asked.

"Well, after Christopher left me to fend for myself," Molly began and laughed at the fallen look on her brother's face, "I got to thinking about what must have been happening at home, so I started back. Ed, Christopher, and I are the only ones who knew I was pregnant when I began the trip east. But we figured it was early enough for me to travel safely. Besides, I thought I'd be able to get there and back long before the baby was due."

"I can't believe I couldn't tell," Candy said, shaking her head.

"Well, you were somewhat preoccupied with Kathryn's wedding," Molly replied.

"Where's Ed?" Jeremy asked as he sat down. The grogginess had returned and he shook his head.

"He had to go see Chief Brandeis about something. I just got in a little bit ago. He told me about the dinner so I rushed on up. Now, what did I interrupt?"

"Jason was just about to propose a toast," Joshua said as he gave Molly a glass of port.

"Yes, I was," Jason stated and stood again. Jeremy remained seated, however, and Jason continued. "Tonight we celebrate a most joyous event. To the new bride…may your new life be filled with laughter and excitement, but most of all, love. And may God grant you many healthy children to give my little brother gray hair!" Laughter exploded around the room as everyone looked at Jeremy. He just shook his head and laughed. Jason came over to him and placed a hand on Jeremy's shoulder. When he spoke again, his tone was subdued. "And thank God he's here to get that gray hair." No one else said anything as they all sat back down. Jeremy nodded, then slowly stood up.

"All right, all right," he said, smiling. "This is a happy occasion. I want to see smiles on everybody." He sat back down and things got back to a normal, cheerful celebration.

"Well, little one," Joshua said, turning to Kathryn, "tomorrow's your day. Are you ready?"

"I hope so, Uncle Josh," she replied.

"Well, you certainly have been a lot calmer than your mother was at her wedding," Biddie commented.

"Well, I think I got over most of the butterflies the first time," Kathryn said with a gentle laugh.

"I was pretty calm, Biddie," Candy said thoughtfully.

"Oh no, you weren't," Molly interjected. "You were almost late in fact."

"Oh?" Jeremy asked, arching his left brow. He hadn't heard this before.

"She kept fiddling with her hair," Molly explained. "She said if her hair wasn't right, she wasn't going to the church."

"That's right!" Biddie confirmed.

"Oh, please, tell me about it," Kathryn said, her eyes dancing.

"I don't think we need to—" Candy began but her daughter cut her off.

"Please? I love to hear these stories!" she said.

"Oh go on, Candy," Jeremy said with a smile. "I would like to hear about it, too."

"All right, I will," Candy replied and began.

Molly ran excitedly into the bedroom, her long, blond hair already falling down from the curly hairdo Biddie had arranged for the freckle-faced youngster.

"Candy! You're going to be late!" she yelled.

"I won't be late because I'm not going," Candy announced, her blue eyes sad but determined.

"Candy!" Biddie exclaimed, unable to believe what she was hearing. "Of course you're going. Why, you and Jeremy have waited two years for this."

"But my hair looks awful," Candy cried, throwing her hands up in exasperation.

"Your hair looks beautiful," Molly said, admiring her lovely sister. Candy's hair was arranged in a rope fashion on top of her head. She'd been trying to arrange a string of pearls in the hairdo but couldn't seem to get it quite right.

"Here, let me do it," Biddie said impatiently. She quickly fashioned the pearls and Candy was finally ready. "Oh Candy, you're a beautiful bride!"

Meanwhile, in the back room at the church, Jeremy was also fidgety and nervous. He'd been dressed for some time now and paced until Jason made him stop. What was taking so long?

"How's about a belt before the old 'I do's'?" Clancey asked as he shoved a whiskey bottle in Jeremy's face.

"No, Cl-Clancey," Jeremy said, pushing the bottle away.

"Well, it couldn't hurt. I'm not nervous," the sea captain said and took a generous swig.

"Jeremy will be fine," Jason said quietly.

"I'm glad s-somebody's c-calm." Jeremy heaved a deep sigh. "Damn! I don't need this st-stuttering now." He looked at his brothers and shook his head, angry at first. No one else said anything right away. Jeremy tugged at his collar then. "This suit…is too tight!"

"Jeremy—" Joshua began with a laugh but Jason interrupted.

"Now, Josh, Jeremy will be all right," he said, patting Jeremy's shoulder. "You and Candy have waited a long time to be together. Just think of the ceremony as…as…" He paused, trying to think of the right words. Jeremy stopped pulling at his collar for the moment.

"Yeah?" he asked.

"As...merely a brief formality, soon over. Besides, you've been looking forward to this day." Jason smiled and looked pleased with himself.

"That's easy for you to say," Joshua said. "You're not the one gettin' married."

"Right!" Jeremy said. Joshua went over to his younger brother and put a comforting hand on his shoulder.

"Jeremy, you went over the vows last night with Reverend Adams. You weren't nervous then."

"Oh, I was nervous, but I guess I knew it was only p-practice. This isn't!" Organ music began to play out in the sanctuary and Jeremy jumped at the sudden sound.

"You'll be fine, bucko," Clancey said as he left.

"Maybe...maybe you're right, Jason," Jeremy said and finally smiled. "I do love Candy and I do want to be married to her. Guess it's normal to act this way, huh?"

"I think so," Jason said quietly.

"Tonight's what you've gotta be nervous about," Josh added.

"Thanks, Josh, I hadn't thought that far ahead," Jeremy said, his voice sarcastic.

"Hey, just trying to help you out."

"I know, Josh. I guess I am nervous about th-that, too."

"Well, it's a little late for a 'special talk' wouldn't you say?" Jason asked, grinning.

"Jason," Jeremy said, blushing to crimson. As the music grew louder, he sighed. "Well, time to go out."

"It'll be over soon. I'm gonna go get the bride," Jason said and slapped Jeremy on the back on his way out.

"Coming?" Joshua asked.

"Yeah, be there in a minute. Go on," Jeremy replied and Joshua left. Jeremy took one last look in the mirror. He ran his fingers through his shining brown hair and blew out a deep breath. His face was moist with nervous perspiration and he quickly wiped it away with his handkerchief. "Time," he reminded himself out loud.

Once at the altar, he relaxed a bit. Corky Masters, his longtime friend, joked with him about what would follow later in the evening. Jeremy blushed but grinned in spite of it. He just listened and offered very little comment. The less he spoke, the better off he'd be, he thought.

Jason smiled and greeted the women as he strode through the dormitory toward Candy's room. She shared a nice-sized room with her brother and sister just off the kitchen. Jason tapped lightly on the door, which was opened right away. Biddie nodded and smiled, allowing him all the way inside.

Candy turned around to face her brother-in-law and Jason's mouth fell open. He'd always thought Candy was a pretty girl, but now, dressed in a lacy white wedding gown, she looked every inch the beautiful woman.

"Oh, Candy, you're beautiful," Jason murmured. "My brother is the luckiest man alive!"

"Really, Jason?" she asked demurely. Candy was not usually shy, but today was special...she wanted to look her very best. She loved Jeremy.

"Really, Candy," Jason assured her. She bent her head and Jason crossed the room to where she stood. He gently lifted her chin up with a finger, causing her to have to look up at him. "I've never seen you prettier. I've heard it said that when someone is in love, truly in love, it shines forth! Well, Candy, you're shining."

"Oh, Jason." Candy couldn't help but laugh then. "You always amaze me."

"How's that?"

"The way you talk sometimes. It seems out of place somehow."

"Well, I do read a lot. Ready?"

"I...yes." Jason held out his arm for her. She dipped in almost a curtsy, then took his arm, grateful for the strength there.

Biddie hurried into the church ahead of the bride and, at her motioning, the organist began playing the music Candy had picked out. Jeremy took his place at the altar and Joshua, his best man, gave him a reassuring smile.

Biddie appeared first in the procession, dressed in a light blue gown with matching ribbons in her curled hair. Molly gently threw flower petals as she came down the aisle, also in a blue gown. Christopher followed, carrying the ring on a satin pillow. He kept trying to stretch his neck, uncomfortable in his suit and tie. Jeremy grinned knowingly at his almost brother-in-law.

A hush fell on the guests as Candy made her entrance, her hand on Jason's arm. Her white silk gown, covered in lace, enhanced her trim, shapely figure. A transparent veil seemed to flow from her hair as she walked. Her eyes locked onto Jeremy's and never wavered.

"Oh, Jeremy," she whispered, blinking back tears that threatened to spill at any moment.

"I love you," he mouthed and cocked his head to one side, smiling. *Candy has to be the prettiest woman in all of Seattle,* he thought.

Jason gently patted Candy's hand as they proceeded up the aisle. He was a dashing figure himself in his dark suit—tall, dark, and handsome. But Candy only had eyes for the attractive man at the altar.

Jeremy was dressed in a dark gray suit, white shirt, and string tie—his usual formal wear. He'd had a brown suit made but someone else had needed it far worse than he, and he gave it away. But he cut a most handsome figure, especially when he smiled. His whole face just seemed to light up and his blue eyes twinkled more than they usually did.

"Welcome to the family, little sister," Jason whispered to Candy as they walked down the aisle. Candy nodded her head, her eyes never leaving Jeremy's. Jason smiled at his youngest brother as he placed Candy's hand in Jeremy's.

"Who gives this woman?" the minister asked.

"I do," Jason replied then backed up. Jeremy and Candy faced Reverend Adams; neither was nervous anymore.

Vows were exchanged in short order but not without a kind of warning from the minister. He left the couple, and everyone else, with the sense of being kind to one another, now and always.

"I do," Candy said in answer to the minister's familiar question.

Jeremy turned to Candy and lifted her veil back. He smiled at the sight of her tears. Blinking back a few of his own, he murmured, "I love you." Not waiting on the minister to give permission to kiss the bride, Jeremy took his wife in his arms, sealing their vows with a tender kiss.

"It was a perfect wedding, wasn't it?" Candy asked with a deep sigh. She looked up into her husband's eyes and smiled. He lowered his head for a gentle kiss, forgetting everyone else for the moment.

"It sounds so romantic," Kathryn said dreamily, interrupting her parents.

"Yes, it was," Molly stated. "You and Steven have kind of followed Jeremy and Candy in a way."

"What do you mean?" Jeremy asked.

"Well, the fire put their wedding plans on hold. It took you and Candy two years to get married. I don't think I know anyone who waited so long."

"Well, there were usually good reasons for the waiting," Candy said. "But we don't need to talk about them now."

"The decorations in the park are beautiful, Mother," Kathryn said. "You got them up so fast."

"I had a lot of help," Candy replied, looking at her husband. "Well, some help, anyway." Jeremy nodded and chuckled.

"I tried," he said.

"Things are much grander now than when we got married," Joshua said, taking Callie's hand.

"It wasn't any less festive or romantic, though," his wife replied. "But it was a wedding to remember."

"How's that?" Steven asked.

"Josh and Callie got married on Clancey's ship," Jeremy said with a laugh. "With Clancey performing the wedding!"

The outside of the S*hamus O'Flynn* was adorned with flowers of all colors, shapes, and smells. The old mule scow seemed reborn. Joshua nervously shifted from one foot to the other. Jeremy smiled knowingly; he'd been nervous like this once...and not all that long ago.

"Josh, let me ask you something," Jeremy said quietly.

"Sure."

"You love Callie, don't you?"

"Well, of course I do," Joshua replied, puzzled. "What kind of question is that?"

"Just checking. I mean, you act like you're goin' to a funeral." He laughed and backed away.

"Yeah, well, I seem to remember *your* wedding, little brother. You weren't exactly calm!"

"Well, I-I..." Jeremy stuttered then lifted his chin up and said, "I was all right once the ceremony got started."

"That you were," Josh said, nodding.

"You will be, too."

"I'm sure I will be." Joshua smiled then added, "I just hope Jason's taking as good o' care of Clancey as you are of me!" They both nodded at that, hoping that Jason's care of Clancey was even better. Joshua hugged his brother; they'd been through a lot together. Jeremy blinked quickly and cleared his throat.

"I bet Callie's beautiful," he said.

"Well, with Candy and Biddie helping her, how can she be anything but beautiful?" Joshua sighed again. "I'll be glad when the ceremony is over. Did your suit fit this tightly?"

"Yeah, it did...still does!" Jeremy laughed.

They both turned at the sound of Clancey's cabin door opening. Jason led the ornery sea dog out, still complaining. They all laughed at him; it wasn't often Clancey allowed himself to be suited up and sober.

Inside the dormitory, Candy and Biddie had been fussing

over Callie as they helped her dress. The bride wasn't nearly as nervous as her assistants, however.

"You two act like this is your wedding day!" she exclaimed.

"Well, I just can't believe you're not nervous at all," Biddie said, her eyes wide. "Why, I would just be a bundle of nerves." She paused then added, "But I wouldn't mind it!"

"Hasn't Corky popped the question yet, Biddie?" Callie asked.

"No, not yet," Biddie said, sighing. "I think he's working up to it. I asked Jeremy to hurry him along, though. If he doesn't ask soon, *I'm* going to ask *him*."

"Oh Biddie, you wouldn't!" Candy almost dared.

"I think she's serious," Callie said, laughing. Biddie stood back and admired Callie.

"There now, I think you're ready."

"Thank you, both of you," Callie replied and looked into the mirror. Her hands shook a little as she adjusted her new glasses. "I am nervous," she said with a light laugh. "I think I would be more so if I didn't have you two around. I am more than a little nervous about one thing though." She started to rub her hands on her skirts but Candy caught hold of them, shaking her head.

"What's that?" Biddie asked.

"Clancey performing the ceremony. I mean, I know Joshua really wants him to do it but—"

"Don't you worry," Candy said firmly. "Jason'll see to it that Clancey is at his best." The women laughed at that. It wasn't often that Clancey was asked to preside over a wedding. But when he did, it was always an event to be remembered...and cherished.

"Well, I hope my—our—wedding is as memorable," Kathryn said when Joshua and Callie finished relating their story.

"It'll be the best!" Steven exclaimed.

"I'd listen to him if I were you," Jeremy said, suppressing

a yawn. "Remember, the vows say to obey!" Candy made a real show out of clearing her throat even though her first inclination was to punch Jeremy's ribs. But since she couldn't do that yet, she had to do something else. Jeremy chuckled, keeping his left arm over his rib cage, just in case. "Funny how women don't seem to like that part," he quipped.

"It's getting late," Jason said, yawning. "I should be getting home...see how Clancey is."

"Tell him hello for me, won't you?" Kathryn asked.

"You bet. Jeremy, get some rest," he said, looking his youngest brother in the eye.

"Don't worry, Jason, I will," Jeremy replied with a smile. He started to stand up but Candy pushed him back down.

"I'll see them out, all right?" she asked, standing.

"Thanks. I'll see all of you tomorrow," he said, nodding. Everyone but Molly headed for the door with Candy.

"Jeremy?" Molly asked, sitting beside her brother-in-law.

"Yes?"

"What's wrong?"

"Wrong? Uh, nothing's wrong. Why?" Molly placed a gentle hand on his and smiled.

"Did something else happen while I was away? I only knew about the fire and I wasn't around long enough for Ed to tell me anything else."

"Well, we did have some trouble," Jeremy replied. He blew out a deep breath before going on. "Kathryn's wedding began as planned but a man she'd met at school, Jerome Douglas, showed up at the church and stopped the wedding. He said she'd been *with* him—um, well, you know.

"Anyway, his presence and accusations confused Steven, and Kathryn called the wedding off. Before we could get Douglas to explain, he disappeared. Shortly after that, the fire started and everyone worked at putting it out. I suppose you've seen how much was destroyed?"

"Yes, I did. But I've never seen so many tents up in one place before. Guess it's hard to keep people down, huh?"

"Guess so. Rebuilding began almost right away."

Candy stood quietly in the hallway, listening to her husband recount the recent events. She knew he would leave nothing out so she stayed out of sight. It was just so hard to hear how she'd almost lost him. Not that it was the first time he'd ever been hurt, but he was older and healing took a lot longer.

"So, what else happened?" Molly asked.

"Douglas didn't leave Seattle. He and I had words at the church and you know how bad my temper can be at times." Jeremy paused and laughed at that.

"I seem to recall something about that."

"Thanks. Well, I put myself in a bad spot and was alone when Douglas finally showed his face again. We argued and my temper got the better of my judgment. I called the man a liar. He was armed but I thought I could make him see reason. He didn't.

"He shot me, twice, and left me for dead. If it hadn't been for the fire's approach, I think he would've f-finished me."

"Dear God," Molly breathed.

"Exactly," Candy said, coming up behind them. Tears glimmered in her soft blue eyes as she put her hands on Jeremy's shoulders.

"You're all right now, though, right?" Molly asked, stunned at this news.

"Oh, sure. It's just gonna take awhile to recover completely, that's all."

"What about this Douglas?"

"He was finally caught and taken to Olympia for trial. Ask Ed about the rest. You've got a good husband, Molly."

"I know. We've been very lucky that he hasn't been seriously hurt on the job. Well, I'd better head on home and talk to my husband." Molly stood up as did Jeremy. He gave her a gentle hug and kiss.

"Would you like me to take you home?" he offered.

"No, Christopher's waiting on me. But thanks. You get some rest, like Jason said."

"See you tomorrow, Molly," Jeremy said, nodding. Candy went to the door with her sister and Jeremy started up the stairs when he heard a noise in the kitchen. Curious, he went in and found one of his son's dogs sniffing around the room.

"Okay, outside with you," Jeremy chuckled and opened the door. The dog whimpered but went out.

Chapter Nineteen

The sun's rays streamed through Kathryn's bedroom window early the next morning, waking her up. She stretched lazily in bed and looked around her room. This was her last day in it, as Kathryn Bolt anyway. In just a few hours, she would be a married woman.

"Mrs. Steven Fairfield," she spoke aloud and wrinkled her nose. "Mrs. Kathryn Fairfield…Kathryn Bolt-Fairfield." She sat up, smiling. She'd known of a few women who had kept their own last names in addition to their husbands'.

"That might not go over very big in Seattle," came her father's voice from her doorway.

"Why not? I mean, we're not far from a new century. Women should be allowed to make decisions for themselves!"

"Don't yell at me. I didn't make the rules," Jeremy defended.

"Well, you are responsible in part."

"How's that?"

"You are a man."

"That's not fair, Kathryn, and you know it," he retorted. He frowned and walked away. Kathryn sighed heavily and got up. Her father was right; it wasn't his fault, exactly. She threw on her robe and hurried down the stairs.

Jeremy heaved a deep sigh as he sat down on the front porch. He'd have to square things with Kathryn, he knew. He didn't want to ruin the biggest day of her life, even if he had nothing to apologize for. Sometimes it was better to concede than argue.

"Hi," Kathryn spoke softly.

"Hello," Jeremy replied.

"May I join you?"

"Sure." Neither spoke again for a couple of minutes. Then, Kathryn looked into her father's deep blue eyes and smiled.

"I'm sorry, Daddy," she said. "You were right, it isn't your fault."

"Well, thank you for that," Jeremy said and patted his daughter's hand. "Things will get better for women, someday. God knows there are probably a lot like you and your mother. Change usually happens slowly though. Try to be patient."

"I'll try, but it is hard sometimes. Mother does so much around the community, but it's almost as if what she and the other women do doesn't matter."

"Yes, I know. It took a very long time for people to warm up to Dr. Wright when she arrived. Even though she saved my life, it was still a long time before she was accepted. I'm not sure she's entirely accepted now."

"I wonder why she never married?" Kathryn mused. "I mean, I know she and Uncle Jason like one another."

"Oh, I don't know. They've had a special kind of friendship, but nothing more. And for them, that seems to be enough. Not everyone feels the need to marry. Jason has the family business and Dr. Wright has her medical practice."

"You're up awfully early this morning," Kathryn said, changing the subject. "I mean, I can understand why I am."

"I suppose I woke up for some of the same reasons you did. I'm a little nervous about having to give you up."

"You aren't giving me up, Daddy," she said, putting an arm around her father's shoulders. "I'll always be your daughter. I love you very much."

"I love you, too." Jeremy patted her hand then stood up. "Better go in and start getting dressed. Candy will be up before long, anyway."

"I think she already is. I heard some movement coming from your bedroom when I came down."

"Oh." Jeremy turned to his daughter who had stood as well. "I really do wish all the best for you and Steven. But don't make fun of me if you see a tear now and then."

"I won't, Daddy, I promise. Well, I'd better go in and help Mother get breakfast started. Jon will be up before we know it."

"You just relax. I'll help your mother."

"Thank you, Daddy…for everything." Jeremy kissed her cheek then went back inside the house.

"Mornin'," Jeremy greeted his wife as he walked into the kitchen a few minutes later. Candy smiled warmly and nodded. "Need some help?" he asked.

"As a matter of fact, yes," she replied. She handed him a teapot. He took it and began filling it with water while Candy started to slice bacon.

"Candy?" he asked.

"Yes?" But Jeremy was silent for a few seconds and Candy stopped what she was doing to look at her husband. "What is it, Jeremy?"

"Don't cry, all right? Cause if you do, I will." He grinned at that and Candy immediately went to his side.

"Oh, Jeremy, I do love you," she whispered. He held her tightly, sighed, and smiled.

"Kathryn does have that—what is it you call it, glow?" he said.

"Yes. I thought I would feel old when this day came, but I really don't. I think I did a little a few weeks ago, though." She stood back, thoughtful. "Maybe Jonathan is the reason," she added.

"I'm not so sure about that," Jeremy chuckled. "I heard about what he did at school the other day."

"Swallowing the string?" Candy said, shuddering. "Oh, I know. I heard all about it from Miss Page. I was set to punish him but that woman carried on so, I just didn't have the heart."

"She does upset easily. I think she'll be glad when Kathryn takes over. I know Miss Essie was happy that someone else could take over the summer lessons, though."

"I think so. Besides, it isn't good for the children to make fun of their teacher, even if she does shock easily."

"I heard Obie's girl told Miss Page that she was the most shockin' person she knew!" Jeremy said, chuckling.

"Yes, and do you know, she hasn't used the word 'shock' since? Kathryn will make a good teacher. She knows all the children."

"Guess we'd better get breakfast ready, huh?" Jeremy asked with a sigh. Candy nodded and turned back to her bacon. Jeremy put the teapot on the stove, looking a little lost. He walked over to the door and, with his hand on the handle, turned back to Candy. "I'm…gonna go outside for a while. Yell if you need me," he said.

"All right. Are you…" Jeremy nodded at Candy's unfinished question and smiled, then went out. Candy sighed and went on with her cooking.

By three o'clock that afternoon, family and friends gathered once more inside the little white church. The mood was as festive as it had been the first time, and a bit more relaxed. This wedding would always be remembered as especially wonderful. The fire had hit most of the citizens very hard but could not dampen their spirit. Kathryn and Steven's vows would reflect that and ensure Seattle's future growth.

"Now I would like to present Mr. and Mrs. Steven—" the

minister began but Kathryn shook her head at him and smiled. He nodded and corrected himself, "Kathryn and Steven Fairfield. May their new life together serve as a symbol of a new beginning for all of us."

"Amen to that!" Jason stated, standing. All the others in the church stood as well as the new couple went down the aisle. The wedding party filed out behind the bride and groom, then everyone else followed suit. Soon, everyone was headed for the park by Elliot Bay for the reception.

Jonathan and Richard lost no time shedding their cumbersome ties and jackets after they'd reached the park. They didn't wait on anyone else either as they began cramming food into their mouths. Candy and Callie exchanged knowing glances as they shook their heads at their sons.

Then, as soon as the happy couple had toasted one another and pictures were taken, all the other men discarded their ties and jackets as well. Soon, music and laughter filled the park, and a contented hum settled over the crowd.

Kathryn and Steven managed to slip away from the group, most of whom didn't even notice they'd left. Kathryn removed her veil as she sat down on the grass. Steven sat beside her and smiled.

"I never thought we'd be able to sneak away," he said. "Don't Jason and Stempel ever quit?"

"What do you mean?" Kathryn asked, puzzled.

"Competing! I mean, they even tried to outdo one another toasting."

"Oh, no. I don't they'll ever quit. I guess I see it as natural."

"Your father is in high spirits today, too. That's good to see."

"Yes, it is." She heaved a deep sigh and her husband put his arms around her. "So much has happened."

"But the bad is behind us now," he said. "We have a lot ahead of us, too. I'm glad you'll be there beside me."

"So am I. I love you, Steven," Kathryn said, smiling. As their lips met, she closed her eyes. She knew she and Steven would have a good life together.

Just as the wedding guests noticed their absence, the happy couple reappeared to thank everyone. The sun had gone down and lanterns had been lit, giving the park an ethereal glow. Kathryn didn't think she'd ever seen a prettier place.

"Well, you two have been gone awhile," Joshua exclaimed and smiled at the blush that came to his niece's face.

"We...uh...just went for a walk," Steven stammered.

"We are married," Kathryn stated with a laugh.

"Yes, I know," Jeremy said, clearing his throat.

"Hey, we've got time for another toast," Jason said loudly.

"No, we'd like to toast all of you," Steven said. "If there's anything left to drink." Someone handed him a glass of champagne and he held it high. "A special thanks to Jeremy and Candy. For having such a beautiful daughter."

"Oh, Steven," Kathryn said shyly.

"May your lives be rich in love," Candy said softly.

"I love you," Kathryn whispered and hugged both her parents in turn, tears seeping out of the corners of her eyes.

"Get outta here, you two!" Jason said with a hearty laugh.

"But I didn't get to make a toast," Aaron Stempel complained.

"A speech, you mean!" Joshua laughed.

"Well, I'll make one when they get back!" Stempel replied.

"Thank you, all of you," Steven said quietly. "I know our wedding heralds both our beginning and Seattle's new life. I feel very blessed to be a part of all of it. Thank you for making me feel that I belong." No one else said a word; Steven's eloquent speech said it all.

Shortly after sunrise the next morning, Kathryn and Steven boarded the steamer that would take them to Victoria, Canada. Although it would be shorter than they would've liked it, a honeymoon was at least possible.

Tearful good-byes were exchanged and the couple continued to wave as the ship pulled out. Then, it was business as usual for everyone else.

"Well, I guess we'd better get back to work," Jason said as the Bolt families walked away from the pier.

"Yes, and we women have a lot of cleaning up to do at the park," Candy said. "That includes you, Jonathan," she added as her son ran to catch up with his cousin.

"Oh, gosh," he whined. Everyone else laughed at his moaning. He had plans to show Richard his new pet—a three-foot-long snake. His parents hadn't seen this new addition yet.

"C'mon, Jon," Richard said, pulling on his cousin's sleeve, "the sooner we help, the sooner we can see Randy."

"Who's Randy?" Joshua asked.

"Just…a friend, Uncle Josh," Jonathan replied. He and Richard quickly took off before they could be asked anything else.

"They're a lot like you and Jeremy were," Jason said to Joshua. "And I'll lay you odds that Randy is not a boy."

"I'd agree with that," Jeremy said, laughing. He turned to Candy then. "See you at supper."

"All right. You sure you should be riding a horse yet?" Candy asked, almost frowning.

"I'll be fine, Candy. Besides, this mare is very gentle." Jeremy grunted a little as he mounted his horse. His brothers had issued similar sounds but they were already astride their mounts. Jeremy grinned and shook his head. "There ought to be a law about gettin' old!" he exclaimed. The women could still hear the men's laughter as they disappeared.

"I'll help with the cleaning," Biddie offered. She climbed into the buggy with Candy, Callie, and Essie.

"You're not going to open the library today?" Callie asked as Candy started the horses forward.

"Melissa is there today," Biddie replied proudly. She and Corky had every right to be proud of their almost grown daughter; she was the only child they'd been able to have. And she was a beautiful girl. "She's taken quite an interest in the books," Biddie went on. "I think she can handle it without her mother for one day."

"I think she just doesn't want Mother in the way!" Essie laughed.

"Peter's helping, huh?" Candy asked, smiling. The women laughed and chatted quietly as they buggy bumped along the road toward the park.

Chapter Twenty

About a week later, Joshua was in Ben's store, waiting on his supply order to be filled, when Ed Bennett came inside. He frowned as he went up to Jeremy's brother.

"It's awfully early in the day to look so worried, Ed," Joshua said, half-joking.

"I'm not really worried, Josh, but surprised," the deputy replied. He handed Joshua a letter. "Read this. I've got to take it out to Jeremy. Know where he is?"

"Yeah, up at, uh, the main office," Joshua said slowly as he read the contents of the letter. "Hang on a minute and I'll go back with you. Jason and I had both better be around when Jeremy reads this."

"I agree. I'll wait on you outside."

"Kevin," Joshua said to the clerk, "send this stuff out to the camp?"

"Sure thing, Josh," the young man replied and Joshua quickly left.

Jeremy poured himself a cup of coffee then sat back at his desk. It felt good to be productive again, he thought. Even if all he was doing was checking over ledger entries.

"Jeremy," Jason acknowledged as he came inside.

"Want some coffee?"

"Sounds good. I'll get it." Jason poured a cup and started to ask Jeremy a question when Joshua and Ed hurried into the office. "Well, Ed, what brings you out?" he asked.

"This," Ed replied, handing the letter to Jeremy.

"What is it?" Jeremy asked as he took the paper.

"Read it...you aren't going to like it," Josh stated. Jeremy shook his head as he read the letter from Olympia's Marshal Thompson.

"I have to testify," he said quietly. He looked up at the others. "In a week."

"Why?" Jason asked, looking at Ed. "I thought you said that wouldn't be necessary."

"I honestly didn't think it would, given the circumstances at the time," Ed defended. "But evidently, Douglas has a lot more political connections than we could have known. I'm sorry, Jeremy."

"It's all right, Ed. There's nothing to be sorry for. In fact, it's probably better that I do appear. I'd better get some kind of statement from the doctors, huh?" Jeremy said, standing.

"Probably be a wise move," Ed replied.

"Well, I'd better get going. They sure didn't give me much notice."

"We'll go with you," Joshua stated.

"No, Josh, you and Jason are needed more here. I'd appreciate it if Jon could stay with you, though, Josh."

"Sure. You gonna take Candy?" Joshua asked.

"I don't think she'd let me leave without her," Jeremy said, grinning.

"Probably not," Jason agreed with a laugh.

"Thanks for bringing this out to me, Ed."

"No problem. I'll be coming along as well. There's no way Douglas is gonna get off on this."

"All right. We'll meet you in town in, say, an hour?"

"I'll be ready. See you there." The deputy left and Jeremy started to leave but turned back to his brothers.

"I'll be fine," he told them.

"You going by ship?" Jason asked.

"No. I think we'll take the buggy. Weather's nice—might as well enjoy the trip."

"Sounds like a plan," Jason stated.

"I'll wire you when it's over, all right?" Jeremy asked then headed for home.

Jeremy stood by the buggy less then an hour later, talking with Ed. Candy had gone into the bakery with Molly, who was going to go with them as well. Jason and Joshua rode up just then.

"What are you doing in town?" Jeremy asked them.

"We're going," Jason said flatly. Jeremy grinned and nodded.

"Good," he replied.

"Where's Candy?" Joshua asked.

"In the bakery. Said I didn't give her enough time to prepare anything to take along."

"Molly's going, too," Ed said, shaking his head. "You'd think we were going to a party."

"Well, it isn't every day we go to Olympia," Candy stated as she and Molly joined the men. "There's nothing wrong with making the best of the situation."

"She has a point," Jason said, laughing.

"Thank you, Jason," Candy said and smiled. Jeremy helped her and Molly into the buggy, then got in himself.

The trip to the territorial capital proved to be very pleasant and uneventful. It was fortunate that Jeremy had wired the marshal of his coming, and how many others would be with him, because hotel rooms were reserved for them. Had notification not been given, the men would have found themselves out in the street. The hotels were all full. The trial itself was not the main draw; the possibility of a hanging was.

"I'll be glad when this is over," Molly said as she unpacked.

"Think Jeremy'll stick around after he testifies?" Ed asked.

"You can bet on it. At least to hear the verdict. This man will be found guilty, won't he, Ed?"

"I would think so. But having his trial here instead of Seattle is definitely an advantage for Douglas."

"Well, I'm hungry. Let's go get the others and eat," Molly said with a laugh.

"You're always hungry."

"Hey, I'm feeding two now."

"That you are. All right, I'm ready." Ed took his pretty wife's hand and went out.

The next morning, Jeremy was up before dawn. He felt comfortable with what he would say, but having to face Jerome Douglas again bothered him. The man had almost killed him and threatened to take his daughter.

A soft knock sounded at the door, breaking Jeremy out of his wonderings. A smile slowly formed as he went to the door, knowing full well who it would be.

"Mornin', Jason, Josh," he said as he opened the door.

"How did you—," Joshua began but Jason interrupted him.

"It'd be the same with any of us, I expect," he said, grinning. "Candy up yet?"

"No," Jeremy said quietly. He came out into the corridor.

"The hotel restaurant is open. How about some coffee?" Joshua asked.

"Sounds good. Let's go," Jeremy replied.

Just after ten that morning, Candy watched as Jeremy took the stand. His testimony was one of the last given but probably one of the most important. Candy listened to her husband recount the entire incident, from Douglas' sudden appearance to the shooting.

"...and you're certain it was Jerome Douglas who shot you?" the defense attorney asked.

"Yes, without a doubt," Jeremy replied calmly.

"You testified that you had moved into the shadows. With all that was going on at the time, wouldn't it have been possible for someone else to have done the deed?"

"No. And I stated that I *tried* to get into the shadows. I didn't make it."

"Mr. Bolt," the lawyer said, turning to face the jury, "my client has served honorably for many years in law enforcement. Why would he jeopardize his reputation by shooting you, an unarmed man?"

"Because he wanted my daughter," Jeremy said firmly. *Here it comes*, he thought. The attorney shook his head in disbelief, still facing the jury.

"Is your daughter that remarkable?" he asked.

"What I think doesn't matter. Douglas thought enough of her to come all the way to Seattle. And I've given the district attorney wires from Dean Crenshaw—"

"Yes, yes, we've seen them, Mr. Bolt." The man finally faced Jeremy, smiling. "Mr. Bolt, would you, by chance, have a photograph of your daughter?"

"Yes, I have one," Candy called from her seat.

"And you are?" the judge asked.

"Mrs. Bolt, Jeremy's wife, Your Honor," she replied.

"Please give the photograph to Mr. Borland," the judge requested. Candy looked at Jeremy, who nodded, then handed the picture over.

"My, you do have a beautiful daughter, Mr. Bolt," Borland stated. "If it please the court, I would like the jury to take a look at this."

"So be it." Borland gave Kathryn's photograph to the jury members who smiled and nodded.

"Your Honor, I would like to find out where this is going,"

District Attorney Waters said, standing.

"Patience, Henry," Borland said, flashing an oh-so-charming smile at the judge. "Your Honor, I'm trying to understand what would have made my client travel hundreds of miles. After looking at Kathryn Bolt's—"

"Um, her name is Fairfield now," Jeremy interrupted softly.

"What was that, Mr. Bolt?"

"I said her name is Kathryn Fairfield now. My daughter recently married."

"Oh, I see. Thank you. As I was saying, I can certainly see why Mr. Douglas was attracted to Kathryn.

"But let's be serious here. Shooting someone over a bit of pretty fluff just isn't in keeping with my client's nature."

"Fluff?" Jeremy asked, almost rising out of his chair. "My daughter is hardly 'a bit of fluff'!" Before anyone else could say anything, Jeremy shouted, "Jerome Douglas tried to kill me and none of your fancy maneuvering can change that!" People started talking at once and the judge's gavel came down hard several times.

"Mr. Bolt," he said loudly, "please sit down and compose yourself. Marshal Thompson requested your presence but another outburst like that, and I'll dismiss you!"

"I'm...sorry, Your Honor," Jeremy said quietly, sitting back down. His face was flushed and moist.

"Hang in there, Jeremy," Joshua whispered.

"Mr. Bolt," Borland said as he came to stand in front of Jeremy, "I do apologize, sir. Are you feeling all right?"

"Yes, I'm fine," Jeremy replied.

"Good. I'm almost finished."

"Thank God," Candy breathed and felt her sister's hand on hers. Molly smiled and nodded.

The testimonies delivered, the jury retired to deliberate the matter. Waters walked out with the Bolts and Bennetts. It would take some time for a verdict to be rendered.

"Up until your testimony, Borland's been able to cast a

favorable light on Douglas," he told Jeremy.

"What do you think now?" Jason asked.

"It's hard to say. I honestly believe Douglas will be found guilty but the incident took place in Seattle, and it has been a while since it occurred. I don't like courtroom theatrics, but I must admit, I think Jeremy's emotional outburst did more good than harm."

"Good," Jeremy sighed.

"Are you all right?" Waters asked.

"Sure," Jeremy replied. "Just talking about it made me realize just how lucky I am to be alive."

"Mr. Waters," a man said as he hurriedly joined the group. "The jury's back. They've already reached a verdict."

"All right! That can only mean guilty," Waters stated, smiling.

"Jerome Douglas, please stand and face the jury," the judge said. Douglas did so. "Foreman, please read your verdict."

"We, the jury, find the defendant, Jerome Douglas, guilty of the attempted murder of Jeremy Bolt of Seattle." Douglas merely stood and listened with no change of expression on his face. The jury foreman continued. "Further, we find the defendant guilty of assault on an officer and escape from jail."

"Thank you, Foreman," the judge said. "Mr. Douglas, have you any words before I pass sentence?"

"No, Your Honor," Douglas stated.

"Very well, then. Your sentence will be death by hanging. And may God have mercy on your soul."

"We'll file an appeal," Borland reassured Douglas.

"What's the point?" Douglas muttered and his blank expression finally gave way to hate. As he was led away, he shot a malicious look Jeremy's way, which made Candy shiver.

"He really is an evil man," Molly said quietly.

"He scares me," Candy admitted. Jeremy took her hand in his.

"It's over," he said.

"Well, for the most part," Waters said, smiling. "Borland wants to appeal."

"Can he do that?" Jason asked.

"Of course. That's the way the legal system works, but Douglas apparently refused."

"So what happens now?" Joshua asked.

"If an appeal isn't filed by ten tomorrow morning, Douglas will hang by noon."

"Don't you think that's a bit dramatic?" Jason asked.

"No. The sooner the better. What's the point of waiting? You gonna wait around?"

"Just as well," Jeremy said, surprising Candy.

"I thought you'd want to head for home as soon as possible," she said.

"I do, but I want to make sure this is really over."

Everyone retired early after dinner that night. Jason and Joshua stayed up and talked for quite a while in their room, however. It had been an interesting experience.

"I think Douglas is getting what he deserves, don't you?" Joshua asked.

"I suppose so. I'm not sure I agree with execution as a means of punishment though," Jason replied thoughtfully. "It seems almost barbaric."

"You think he should've gone to prison?"

"I don't know, Joshua. I just don't know."

"Jeremy will stay for the hanging."

"Yes, I'm sure he will. It won't be the first he's seen, but it'll stay with him the rest of his life. That I'm sure of."

"I think it'll stay with all of us."

"Good night, Josh," Jason said, yawning. He stretched out on his bed and closed his eyes.

"'Night," Josh replied and did likewise.

No appeal was filed and a large crowd gathered around the gallows. In fact, the atmosphere was festive; shops were closed but food and beverages were available on the street. It was as if a holiday had been declared.

"I'd never let Jonathan see this," Candy said. "I can't believe people have their children here."

"Guess the people here are probably used to this," Jason stated. "The outcome would have been the same in Seattle."

"You think so, Jason?" Jeremy asked.

"The trial would have been much shorter, though," Joshua said. Jason started to say something else when the crowd suddenly quieted. Douglas was led out in the streets; he slowly ascended the steps to the gallows. Jeremy frowned and swallowed several times. He was glad now that he hadn't eaten any breakfast.

A minister spoke quietly, then a hood was placed over Douglas' head. Then the noose. The executioner looked for the sign from the judge, who gave a quick thumbs-down signal.

The silence that permeated the throng of people was broken only by the sound of the trap door opening. Jeremy felt his stomach retch as he watched Douglas' body jerk then go slack as death came quickly.

"Oh, God," he whispered.

"Amen," Jason said.

"Well, let's go home," Candy said as she took Jeremy's hand.

"Yes," he said, nodding. "It's time."

"Jeremy?" Joshua asked. Jeremy looked up and saw Joshua's extended hand. Jeremy placed his hand on top, then Jason added his. Candy and Molly sighed collectively and, despite what had just taken place, they managed to smile.

Chapter Twenty-one

Although life was far from normal, people did begin to settle into routine patterns after a while. The fire had done a lot of damage but reconstruction went on at a fairly fast pace.

About a month later, Jeremy was working full-time again. He had been warned to still take things easier than before, and for once, he'd conceded. He felt lucky just to be alive.

Jeremy and his crew were busily planting tree seedlings on a hilltop logging site one afternoon. It was part of the Bolts' continuing reforestation project. Nature gave bountifully to them and replanting was just one way they could give back. Jonathan Bolt had instilled that ethic in his sons, and they had seen the wisdom of following it.

"Why don't you take a break, Jeremy?" Buddy Ryan asked. Jeremy was bent over as he patted the seedling into the place. He sat up and nodded.

"Good idea," he replied, grinning. He started to say more when he caught sight of Aaron Stempel heading up the hill in their direction. Jeremy stood up and brushed himself off, wondering what the sawmill owner was doing this far out of town.

"Well, Aaron, what brings you out so far?" he greeted Stempel.

"Great news!" Stempel shouted, but he didn't dismount. "Where's Jason?"

"Over at the main office. Why?"

"Just meet me over there." Stempel wheeled his horse around and took off, leaving behind a bewildered but curious Jeremy Bolt. Jeremy sought out his foreman and gave instructions to continue without him. Then he quickly mounted his horse and headed for the main camp.

Jeremy quickly entered Jason's office to find Joshua already there, waiting to hear the earth-shattering news. Stempel stopped his busy pacing when he saw Jeremy. Jason sat quietly behind his desk, smiling amusedly. He'd not seen Stempel this out of sorts in years.

"Have I missed anything?" Jeremy asked.

"No," Jason replied. "All right, Aaron, we're all here. Now, what's your news?"

"Statehood," Stempel said simply, quietly.

"We've heard that before," Joshua said, shrugging. He looked at his brothers, who seemed to be of the same opinion. Rumors of Washington becoming a state had been spread frequently through the years. Still, Aaron Stempel was not a man easily swayed by idle gossip.

"This time it's going to happen," Stempel said forcefully.

"What?" Jason asked, slowly rising to his feet. "Are ya sure? I mean—"

"It's true, Bolt," Stempel interrupted. "Roberts got a call from the governor this afternoon. He said the connection was noisy, but he understood every word." Telephones were still a novelty in the West and Seattle was only linked up with Tacoma and Olympia. And only those who could afford it had one as of yet. Jason shook his head; he didn't much like them. He was all for progress, but telephones were definitely an oddity to him.

"When?" Joshua asked.

"The sixth of November...this year!" Stempel replied.

"Well, that gives us almost four months to plan a celebration," Jason said, grinning now.

"Is that all you ever think about, Bolt?" Stempel asked. He paused a moment then smiled, an eagerness gleaming in his eyes. "Seattle's never seen a party like the one we're going to throw!" he added.

"I don't know about you guys, but I'm gonna go tell my wife," Jeremy said as he headed for the door. Joshua followed right behind.

"Good thinkin'," he said. "I'll go tell Callie. Plan to be at my house tonight for supper."

"Are you sure she'll want to feed this bunch?" Jason asked with a laugh.

"I'm sure. See ya later." As he and Jeremy left, Stempel prepared to leave as well.

"Well, guess I'd better be heading back to the mill," he said.

"Josh included you, you know," Jason said quietly.

"I know. And I'll be there."

"Thanks for the news, Aaron. Our friends and neighbors can certainly use good news about now."

That night, after dinner had been eaten, the men headed for the sitting room for drinks. The women cleaned up the kitchen, but for once, the chore was enjoyable. They chatted happily about Washington becoming a state. While Candy was excited, she was apprehensive as well.

"You know, ladies," she began, "we'll have to have a serious talk with our politicians. Women can't vote in national elections yet. Statehood could mean the end of our local voting rights as well."

"Well, we can't put up with that," Biddie stated.

"You're right, Candy," Callie said. "We'll just have a little talk with Mayor Roberts next week." They all laughed and finished their cleaning. Once the ladies set their minds to do something, it got done. And the mayor was well acquainted with the "delicate" sex's ability to be outspoken on all issues.

The women soon joined the men and voiced their opinions on the coming of statehood. Every single man gathered there howled with laughter. But Candy didn't think what the women had said was funny.

"Jason Bolt!" she shouted.

"Doesn't this remind you of something?" Jeremy asked as he wiped his face. He tried to stop laughing but he just couldn't.

"Well, we've certainly come a long way...or have we?" Jason said. He stifled another laugh as he turned to Candy. "Candy, your views will, of course, be presented to the political body. It's just that you've reminded us of all those proclamations the brides used to present us with."

"Well, we meant every word," Candy stated, her eyes flashing.

"We certainly did," Biddie chimed in. She looked around the room and began to laugh, which got everyone else going again as well. The laughter finally died down and Jason made a startling revelation.

"You know, I have just come to the realization that our new courthouse sits on the old dormitory site. Pretty fitting, wouldn't you say?" he asked.

"I think you're right, Bolt!" Stempel said, nodding. He stood and turned to the women. "Thank you for a lovely meal and a most enjoyable conversation. But it's late and tomorrow's another business day."

"Aaron's right, it is late," Jason agreed. As everyone prepared to leave, Jeremy couldn't help but say one more thing about Washington's impending statehood.

"Maybe we'll get the railhead in here next," he said excitedly.

"And maybe the city will finally get enough money to keep the university going," Candy added.

"Maybe," Joshua said. "Richard and Jon might just be the

first of the family to go and be able to finish."

One by one, the families filed out of the house. The children tried to prolong the parting, of course, but their parents won out in the end.

"Statehood," Jeremy murmured as he got ready for bed.

"Yes," Candy said quietly. "There will be a lot of changes once we're a state." Jeremy looked up at his wife then.

"And not all for the better, I'm afraid," he said. "But women have been trying to get the federal vote, Candy. Maybe it won't be that much of a struggle."

"It's not just that," she replied, sitting beside her husband. "I mean, women have worked just as hard as the men have to help this country grow. Now, we're going to lose our voice."

"I know it doesn't seem fair, but I'm sure you won't give up."

"No, I don't suppose we will," Candy sighed.

"If you ever gave up, on anything, I'd worry," Jeremy said, grinning.

"Oh, Jeremy." Candy smiled then and shook her head. She climbed into bed and snuggled close to Jeremy. "I'm glad we'll be a state, and don't you worry, I'm not about to give up."

Jason and Stempel slowly rode around Seattle's new town square, amazed at how quickly the new buildings were going up. And masonry, not wood, was the building material of choice.

"Seattle is a great place to live," said Jason. "Agreed?"

"I agree to that," Stempel said, nodding. "This catastrophe could have ruined everything we've all worked so hard to build. But lookin' around now—well, there is something to be said about the spirit we have here."

"Statehood...at last," Jason said, shaking his head. "You know, maybe Jeremy's right about Seattle getting the railhead." Stempel nodded in agreement; it would be about time.

Chapter Twenty-two

Jason and Stempel strolled down the new wooden walkway toward Perkins' General Store. Ben had wanted to have a special celebration, inviting only those people who had been a part of Seattle's original beginnings. As the two men walked, they waved to people going by. Seattle was definitely coming back.

Emily Perkins greeted the invited guests with a smile. It had taken a couple of months to get the family business up and running again, but with the help of their friends, they were fully operational once more, although they had been open only off and on for a while already.

"Well, looks like a full house," Ben said, coming up behind his wife.

"Almost. Have you seen Jeremy and Candy?" Emily asked.

"Not yet, but Jason said they were on their way."

"Oh, good."

"Go on inside and I'll wait on them." Emily nodded and went inside the store. Ben heaved a contented sigh as he looked up at his storefront.

"Why, Mr. Perkins, don't you look handsome today?" a woman stated and Ben turned her way.

"Thank you, Miss Lane," he replied, almost blushing. Miss Lane owned and operated one of Seattle's more accepted brothels.

"Say hello to your lovely wife, won't you?"

"I'll, uh, do that."

"Well, see you around," she said, and with a *swish* of her satin skirts, she left.

"What was that all about?" Jason asked, startling Ben.

"She, uh, just stopped by to say hello, that's all."

"I see. Well, you are neighbors, in a way, aren't you?" Jason smirked and Ben shook his head. Jason knew Ben Perkins was as faithful as the day was long, but it was still fun to get him flustered. Bold women did that to the store owner.

"Ah, Jason, I don't know why I let your teasing get to me," Ben said. "She is a pretty woman, though, isn't she?"

"She is that. Maybe I'll go give her a hand later; they do have some cleaning going on." Jason laughed and patted Ben on the back. "Go on in. There's no telling when Jeremy and Candy will get here."

"Maybe you're right. He knows to come on in." Ben went back inside with the eldest Bolt brother, laughing.

"Candy, I'm tellin' ya, it's not going to do any good to start something again," Jeremy almost yelled at his wife.

"We're not going to start anything, Jeremy," Candy called out from the bedroom. She was busy putting a gift together for Ben and Emily while Jeremy paced downstairs. She said no more as she hurried down the stairs. "I'm ready now," she said.

"Candy, you aren't going to win, you know. Miss Lane

and her girls won't leave Seattle."

"We'll see."

"I give up!" Jeremy threw up his hands in defeat. Once outside, he shook his head as he helped Candy into the buggy.

"Well, that was easy," she remarked as Jeremy started the horse forward.

"What I think doesn't matter anyway. But whether you like it or not, those women do serve a purpose."

"Jeremy, immorality is not a real purpose," Candy said loudly. She cast a wary eye at her husband, frowned, then shook her head.

"Candy, have you ever considered that it may not be your place to judge these women?" Jeremy's voice was quiet now.

"I'm not judging them," she replied but shifted uncomfortably in her seat. *I am doing just that*, she thought. "We'll just have a little talk with them, that's all."

"You've had talks with them before. What good did it do?"

"Actually, I think it did do some good. Three of the girls are now married."

"Guess I'll never learn." Jeremy laughed then. He looked at his wife and his blue eyes twinkled again. Candy smiled and nodded. Jeremy was hers and hers alone, she knew. He was only trying to have a sense of fair play about the issue.

They pulled up alongside the store and Jeremy sighed. He knew they were the last guests to arrive. He grinned; Ben and Emily wouldn't think anything about it.

Jeremy was about to help his wife down when two rather buxom women stepped in front of him. He smiled at them and nodded his head.

"Mornin', ladies," he said.

"Mr. Bolt," one replied, giggling.

"Mrs. Bolt," the other acknowledged Candy.

"Hattie," Candy returned and even smiled. "Please tell Miss Lane to expect us around three, won't you?"

"Of course," Hattie answered.

"Thank you."

"You, um, you still cleaning up?" Jeremy asked.

"Why, yes, we are. We could use some...manly help," Hattie said and touched Jeremy's hand, then left with the other girl.

"Jeremy," Candy said, smiling sweetly.

"What?" he asked absently, then jerked his head around. "Oh, sorry, Candy." He helped her down without another word, but his face tinged pink. Candy tried not to smile but it was too late. "Something f-funny?" Jeremy asked.

"No, nothing," Candy said and went inside the mercantile. Jeremy followed close behind, shaking his head.

Just before three that afternoon, Candy, Biddie, Callie, Essie, and some of the others from the Seattle Civic Delegation practically marched down the walkway toward Miss Lane's Emporium. They were armed with brooms, mops, and buckets.

"Here they come, Miss Lane!" one of the girls shouted after she spotted the group. "But they've got stuff to clean with."

"What?" Millie Lane asked. She opened the door of the brothel to look out. "Well, I'll be!"

"Miss Lane," Candy greeted the owner. "Our men said you needed help cleaning, so we decided to come."

"Well, thank you, Mrs. Bolt."

"This doesn't mean we accept your...line of work," Candy went on.

"No, I didn't think it would."

"However, you and your girls did help out during the fire." Candy paused as Biddie snickered. "At the relief tents," she added.

"Oh my, yes, you were a big help," Biddie managed.

"Anyway, we wanted to help you out now," Candy said.

"Will any of the men be along as well?" one of the girls asked. No one replied and she added, "There are some heavy pieces of furniture to move. I don't think we can do it."

"Don't you worry about that," Jason Bolt's loud voice sounded. He nodded his head at the women. "Ladies," he greeted.

"Jason," Millie said, smiling now.

"Well, we didn't want you to think we men didn't want to help," he went on. Candy pressed her lips together as she watched her husband, Joshua, and even Clancey join them. "Now, show us what you need done," Jason said.

"Yes, please do," Candy said, holding her head up.

"I'll, uh, help you ladies out," Jeremy said, taking the bucket out of his wife's hands.

"Thank you," Callie said as she looked Joshua in the eye. He grinned and went inside with Jason and Clancey.

"I'm proud of you," Jeremy whispered to his wife.

"For what?" Candy asked. She motioned to the others to go on in, leaving her and Jeremy alone.

"For helping out."

"Well, what did you expect?"

"You know what I expected."

"People can talk while they clean," Candy stated and went inside. Jeremy rolled his eyes upward and chuckled.

"Well, why don't we call it a day?" Millie Lane said as she looked around. "It's almost ten and I'm sure everyone's tired."

"And hungry," Jason said.

"We're prepared for that," Hattie said. "Please join us for a late supper, all of you."

"Thank you, I think we will," Candy replied.

"I thought I smelled something delicious earlier," Stempel said as he went to wash up. He and several other men had joined the others earlier in the day.

Very little was said over the meal, but Jeremy kept watching his wife. He knew she couldn't leave without saying something. But Candy merely ate and smiled. When the dinner was over, she did speak.

"Can we help you with the dishes?" she asked Millie.

"No, please, you've done so much," Millie replied. "We'll clean up. We do appreciate all your help."

"You're welcome," Candy said, nodding. "Jeremy?"

"Huh?" he asked, startled.

"Let's go home. I'm sure the ladies are tired and want to get to bed, too."

"Uh, yes, all right. Good night," he said and followed his wife out.

"It was a good day," Candy said as she pulled her nightgown over her head.

"Uh-huh," Jeremy said, crawling into bed. Candy had been very quiet all the way home. "Candy?" he asked.

"Yes?"

"You wanna tell me what I missed?"

"I'm not sure I know what you mean." She got into bed, trying not to smile.

"The conversations I heard at Millie's were normal...not preachy."

"Oh, well, I'm sure we'll have other talks."

"I see. Today was kind of a truce, huh?"

"I suppose. You tired?"

"Yes."

"Real tired?"

"I guess so. We did a lot of work and...everyone else...would be...tired," Jeremy said slowly as what had transpired at the brothel finally hit him. "I get it now," he said, grinning, "sleep!"

"One night, anyway," Candy remarked. Jeremy chuckled and pulled his wife close to him. "Thought you were real tired," she whispered.

"I am, good night," he said, yawning. Candy poked him in the ribs. "Ow!" he complained, but his lips covered hers. She sighed and closed her eyes as she felt his desire.

Suddenly, she sat up and Jeremy opened his eyes. He pulled her back down but she refused.

"What's the matter?" he asked as he caressed her back.

"Maybe the other men weren't that tired, either," she said. Jeremy sighed heavily and rolled away from Candy. "Jeremy?"

"Good night," he muttered.

"Good night?" she echoed. Jeremy turned back to her then.

"Candy, not everything's gonna change," he said. "This is one area you should give up on."

"Lottie never had any girls."

"No, but she almost did. Jason was gonna go after some fancy women first."

"He was?"

"Yep. That's what the men wanted."

"Including you?"

"Candy, I was a kid."

"Including you?" she repeated.

"Yes, I guess I did." Candy was silent and looked away from him for a moment. Jeremy went on before she could say any more. "But Miss Essie came inside the saloon and made the men realize the kind of women they really wanted. And Lottie drove the point home.

"Then we went after proper ladies...you, Candy. The moment I saw you, I knew Lottie was right." Candy looked into her husband's deep blue eyes and finally smiled.

"I know. I think I loved you from the start." Jeremy pulled her back down, and this time, she went. "Oh, Jeremy, sometimes I'm so pig-headed!"

"Oh, now and then," he said, chuckling and he held her close. But the war between the women was far from over, he knew.

Chapter Twenty-three

By the first of November, people began making preparations for a grand celebration...statehood. Every day they waited for word from Olympia, and every day that passed without news, Seattle's citizens were disappointed.

On the fifth day of the month, the day before Washington was supposed to be admitted into the Union, Jason and Stempel were called into the mayor's office. Roberts was on the telephone as the two men sat quietly.

"Well, it seems that someone at the governor's office didn't get the state charter signed and submitted in time," he said after hanging up the telephone.

"So what does that mean?" Jason asked. "No statehood?"

"No, just a delay. The governor signed the proper papers and we should hear something in a few days. Thanks for coming down so fast, Jason, Aaron."

"You know you're going to have to tell everyone about this," Stempel stated.

"I know, I know. You two willing to help get the word out?"

"Of course," Jason replied, standing. "I'll get word to my brothers and we'll start letting people know."

Joshua was working on accounts when Jason walked into the office at the main Bolt camp. The scowl on his big brother's face let Joshua know something wasn't right.

"No statehood?" he asked.

"It's...coming," Jason replied. "We just don't know when. Where's Jeremy?"

"He got a message to go home." Joshua laughed. "I think Kathryn had some news for the family."

"Jeremy's gonna be a grandfather?"

"Think so. C'mon, let's go find out." Jason laughed and he and Joshua quickly left.

Candy was hugging her daughter when Jeremy rushed into the kitchen of his house. When he saw the familiar smile on both women's faces, he was stunned.

"Kathryn...you-you're-you're not...not..."

"I am!" Kathryn stated, putting an end to her father's stuttering. "You are going to be a grandfather! Congratulations!"

Jeremy sat down, overwhelmed. Both Kathryn and Candy laughed at his reaction.

"Steven is a lot like Dad," Kathryn remarked. "Dad?" she asked.

"Grandfather? Grandpa? Papa?" Jeremy muttered, trying the title on for size. Then he looked up at the women. "Hey, where's Steven? Is he all right?"

"All right?" Candy asked, puzzled. "Jeremy Bolt! You act as if this is something terrible. This is wonderful. We're going to...be...grandparents. Oh..." Her voice trailed as she sat down as well. The fact that she was going to be a grandmother finally hit her. It was Jeremy's turn to laugh now.

"Yeah...Grandma," he laughed. Then he stood up and hugged his daughter. "Are you all right? Where *is* Steven?"

"I'm fine. And Steven is around Seattle somewhere, telling his friends. Now, let's go tell my uncles!"

"We're here!" Jason bellowed as he and Joshua ran inside. "This is wonderful news!"

"Well, Grandpa Jeremy!" Joshua exclaimed and slapped his brother on the back. Jeremy nodded and chuckled.

"Hey, where's the lucky father?" Jason asked.

"Somewhere in town by now, I expect. He went to tell his friends the news about the baby. He's so excited," Kathryn said, and was hugged by both uncles.

"Well, this should put gray in that hair now," Jason told Jeremy, who only sneered at him. Joshua was standing right next to Jeremy and looked down.

"I think I see gray already," he said.

"Ha, ha. You're just jealous," Jeremy said as he made a face at his brothers.

"I can wait," Joshua said and grinned. "Got any coffee, Candy?"

"Of course. Hungry?" Candy asked.

"Whatcha got?"

"Oh, I've still got some apple pie from last night."

"Sounds good." Candy shook her head and patted Joshua's shoulder as she went by. Jason suddenly remembered *his* news and got everyone's attention.

"I hate to spoil the celebration, but I'm afraid Mayor Roberts received some...news today concerning statehood." No one else said anything as they waited for Jason to continue. "Seems as if the state charter wasn't signed and submitted in time for tomorrow's admission. So, what this means is a delay. The mayor is going to let us know when the new date is. Until then, we need to help spread the word to our friends and neighbors."

"Well then, I guess that means the ladies won't have to do so much cooking," Candy said and everyone quietly chuckled.

"I hope that doesn't mean no supper tonight?" Jeremy asked.

"Always thinkin' with your stomach, huh?" Joshua said with a laugh.

"You don't seem to be underfed, Brother!" Jeremy replied, sneering.

"Nope, I'm not complaining," Joshua said and bit into his pie.

"I'll take a slice of that, Candy," Jason said as he sat down.

"There you go, Jason, that's the last of it."

"You gonna make another?" Jeremy asked as he licked his lips.

"I'll make you one, Dad," Kathryn stated and hugged him.

"Thank you. Just make sure my brothers aren't anywhere nearby," Jeremy said then laughed. "Come on, I'll help you find Steven." Kathryn nodded then she and her father left.

Early the next day, a crowd gathered around the entrance to the mayor's office, waiting for word on statehood. Practically everyone wore thick coats and warm hats as it was a bitterly cold day for November.

Inside the mayor's office, Roberts was on the telephone with the governor's office, and the Bolt brothers and Stempel waited patiently. Roberts broke into a smile as he concluded his call.

"It's done," he stated. "The new admission date will be the eleventh of this month. The governor assured me that everything is on the up and up, and Washington will be a state in short order. The forty-second state of the United States of America!" At first, nothing was said. Then, one by one, the cheers started. Everyone in the room rushed out to tell those outside the good news.

A few days later, Ben Perkins was talking with Jason when the telegraph began to click. Jason smiled and finished putting canned goods in a box. Ben shook his head; he'd been deciphering telegraph messages for years now. He'd be glad when everyone could afford a telephone.

"Ah, wouldn't you know that thing would start?" he said. "Excuse me, Jason." Jason nodded and started to leave when Ben yelled excitedly. "Jason! You better get the mayor right away. I think this is it!"

"I'm on my way," Jason said and was out the door as Ben carefully wrote down the incoming message.

"Roberts!" Jason bellowed as he ran into the mayor's office. "Get over to Ben's now! The message is coming in!"

"Right behind you," Roberts said excitedly and the two men ran out.

Not long after, Roberts stood outside Perkins' establishment, waiting patiently for the quickly gathering throng of citizens to settle down. News had spread very fast about the telegram from Olympia.

"Our delegate to Congress, John Wilson, wired Governor Moore that Washington is now a state!" Roberts practically yelled. Shouts erupted all over and the mayor held up his hands, indicating he had more to say. People quieted down and listened.

"Mr. Wilson says, 'Washington is now a state. I saw the president sign the proclamation.' And, he signed it with a pen made of gold...gold mined right here in Washington! Elisha P. Ferry will be inaugurated on November 18th as the first governor of the great state of Washington, in Olympia!" The crowd cheered even louder and plans were already being formulated to send a delegation from Seattle to Olympia to be on hand for the inauguration.

A couple of days before the inaugural, the Bolt brothers gathered at Stempel's office, laying out their plans for the trip to Olympia. All four men were excited as they discussed matters.

"Well, we've certainly waited a long time for this," Jason said.

"You're not wrong there, Bolt," Stempel replied. "We really have come a long way."

"While you get things together here, I'm goin' after my family," Jeremy said. "Josh?"

"I guess I'd better go see if Callie is ready, too. See you in town, Jason." Jason and Stempel nodded, and Joshua and Jeremy left to get their families.

The morning of the long-awaited event was bitterly cold but people refused to stay away. Olympia, forever the area's capitol, was full to overflowing with delegations from all over the new state. The group from Seattle waited along with other Washingtonians for the new governor's address.

Everywhere, banners were held up. There were even two, of very different language, posted to the front of the capitol building. One read: "Isaac I. Stevens, first in the hearts of the people of Washington Territory; E.P. Ferry, first in the hearts of the people of the state of Washington."

Another one read, in Indian language: "Chinook quanism ancotty, alti chee chaco alki (living hitherto in the past, we now begin to live in the future)."

The retiring territorial governor finished his brief speech and extended his hand to the new governor. The spectators cheered loudly and for several minutes.

Once the crowd quieted, Ferry spoke about the long struggle for statehood. While his words were eloquent, and some even understood what he was getting at, the people were more interested in celebrating.

"To those whose hair has grown white beneath this sky," Ferry began, "to those who planted the standard of civilization and Christianity within its borders; to those, the ever-to-be-remembered pioneers, it is an event of transcendent interest; to those it is the consummation of hopes long deferred yet ever renewed."

"Short and sweet," Jason whispered, grinning.

"Quite," Candy agreed, nodding. She looked at her husband whose face was blank at first, then he smiled with a nod.

A cannon roared with approval and cheers erupted once more. Then more cannon fire from the Tacoma camp; Tacomans were fond of roaring cannons. All the delegations tended to keep to themselves, but a few brave souls managed to mingle outside their own groups.

Jason, Stempel, Joshua and his family, and Jeremy and his

family decided to head back to Seattle by late afternoon. They'd seen what they'd come to see. Now, they were anxious to get home and share with the other citizens of Seattle.

Jason came riding up beside Joshua's buggy and his brother promptly pulled his horse up. Jeremy was busy talking to Candy and almost didn't see Joshua stopped.

"I wonder what's wrong?" Jeremy asked and hopped down. He quickly joined his brothers. "What's going on?" he asked them.

"Gettin' hungry," Jason said, grinning. "How about we stop soon?"

"Sounds good," Jeremy replied and ran back to his family. It wasn't long before they found a suitable spot and everyone piled out. The children were especially glad for the stop. Richard and Jonathan chased one another, but remained in full view of their parents.

"Well, we're a state," Jeremy said, sighing. "I'm not sure I understood everything the governor said, but I am sure of one thing: the toughest task is still ahead—seeing what our new politicians will do." Everyone laughed at his remarks; they were all too true.

"I'm afraid you're right, little brother," Jason stated. "But we have to hope for the best and make sure our voices are heard."

"Well, one thing's for sure," Joshua said, taking a bite of chicken.

"What's that, Joshua?" Candy asked.

"We're gonna feel the hand of the big boys in Washington City now."

"What exactly does that mean?" Callie asked.

"What it means is this: we women will have a fight on our hands. Isn't that right, Jason?"

"I'm afraid so, Candy. But I'm confident you'll be letting *your* voice be heard." They all laughed at that, knowing the women were far from the weaker sex. The women had struggled along with the men in creating the dream that had become Seattle...and the state of Washington.

About the Author

Charlotte Fox earned a bachelor's degree from Arizona State University. She has won numerous awards for writing in the mystery and romance-suspense genres. Currently a screenplay based on *Spirit of the Northwest* is in production. She now resides in Wisconsin with her husband and daughter.